MEETING PRINCE CHARMING

A Bookish Book Club Novel

EMMA LEA

Cover design by Michelle Birrell
Book design and production by Michelle Birrell
Cover photograph licensed by Adobe Stock

❀ Created with Vellum

OTHER BOOKS BY EMMA LEA

This is Emma Lea's complete book library at time of publication, but more books are coming out all the time. Find out every time Emma releases a book by going to her website (www.emmaleaauthor.com) and signing up for her Newsletter.

SWEET ROMANCES

These are romantic tales without the bedroom scenes and the swearing, but that doesn't mean they're boring!

The Young Royals

A Royal Engagement

Lord Darkly

A Royal Entanglement

A Royal Entrapment

A Royal Expectation

A Royal Elopement

A Royal Embarrassment

A Very Royal Christmas

A Royal Enticement

Bookish Book Club Novellas

Meeting Prince Charming

Meeting the Wizard of Oz

Meeting Santa Claus

SWEET & SEXY ROMANCES

In my Sweet & Sexy Romances I turn up the heat with a little bit of sexy.

No swearing, or very minimal swearing, and brief, tasteful and not too graphic bedroom scenes.

Love, Money & Shoes Series

Walk of Shame

Standalone Novels

Amnesia

HOT & SEXY ROMANCES

Hot & Spicy Romances turn the heat way up. They contain swearing and sexy scenes and the characters get hot under the collar.

Recommended for 18+ readers

TGIF Series

Girl Friday

Black Friday

Good Friday

Twelve Days

Twelve Days of Christmas - Her Side of the Story

Twelve Days of Christmas - His Side of the Story

Collins Bay Series

Last Call

The Christmas Stand-Off

Standalone Novels

Learning to Breathe

Romantic Suspense

Hide & Seek

<u>TOO HOT TO HANDLE ROMANCES</u>

These are definitely 18+ reads and contain graphic sex scenes and high level swearing – not for the faint of heart

<u>The Young Billionaires</u>

The Billionaire Stepbrother

The Billionaire Daddy

The Billionaire Muse

The Billionaire Replacement

The Billionaire Trap

Christmas with the Billionaire

<u>Music & Lyrics</u>

Rock Star

Songbird

Strings

Sticks

Symphony

<u>The Playbook Series</u>

In Like Flynn

Manscaping

<u>Serendipity Trilogy</u>

The Wrong Girl

The Right Girl (coming soon)

The Only Girl (coming soon)

ABOUT THIS BOOK

Georgie Danners is a nerd and proud of it. She is also the proud owner of Bookish, a bookshop/cafe in the small Northern Tablelands town of Oxley Crossing. She loves all things books and movies and computer games and has a soft spot in her heart for one of Australia's greatest exports, Connor Faulkes, aka Prince Charming.

Connor Faulkes, movie star, is happy to spend the next six weeks with his Gran while she recuperates from a fall that resulted in a broken leg. It would give him an opportunity to have some down time before the filming on his next movie starts and he might even be able to squeeze in some rock climbing if he's really lucky. What he did not expect was to run into, literally run into, a quirky woman who captures his heart with her adorable dorkiness and cute smile.

But can the Prince Charming of the RomCom world really find the girl of his dreams in a shy, socially awkward bookshop owner who would rather live life vicariously through the characters between the pages she reads? Or is this budding romance destined to be a box office fail?

Meeting Prince Charming takes place in a fictional town in the Northern Tablelands of New South Wales in Australia. The Northern Tablelands, also known as the New England Tablelands, are situated on a plateau in the Great Dividing Range and are the largest highland area in Australia with an elevation of 1,000 metres and more above sea level. Oxley Crossing takes its name from John Oxley, an Australian explorer who passed through the area in 1818.

Australia happens to be in the Southern Hemisphere, and as such, the seasons may be different to what you're used to. Summer in Australia is at Christmas (December to February), the new school year begins in February and finishes in December and the final year of high school is Grade 12. Tertiary education is usually University or TAFE (Technical And Further Education) or other vocational training.

Boxing Day is celebrated on December 26 and started as the traditional day for servants and tradesmen to receive their 'Christmas Box' from their bosses or employers. It is a public (or bank) holiday and has become synonymous with big retail stores sales.

Other fun facts about Australia:
- We use the metric system for measurement (millimetres, centimetres, metres and kilometres)
- We use Celsius for temperature (30°C is equal to 86°F)
- we use dollars and cents for currency
- Yes, we have some of the most dangerous creatures on earth living in our country
- No, we don't have koalas, kangaroos and wombats as pets
- we like our beer cold (and our wine too)

This book contains Australian spelling and you may even stumble across a few colloquial slang words - a quick Google search should be able to provide a meaning if you're unsure.

I wrote this book for me :) But I dedicate it to all those other women out there who like to escape into romance novels and dream about Prince Charming too.

❄ I ❄

Georgie Danners pulled her car to a stop by the kerb and turned off the engine. She stared out the passenger window at the house and then looked down at her phone to double-check the address. She had known Dawn for ages; she was a regular customer at Bookish and a loyal member of the Bookish Book Club, but this was the first time Georgie had ever been to her house. It was a beautiful Federation style house, with red brick and tile, white mullioned windows and white trim. The house was not unusual for the town of Oxley Crossing, as the abundance of well-maintained Federation homes kept the town on the tourist maps. What was surprising was that this particular house was also rumoured to be the house in which Conner Faulkes had grown up. Connor Faulkes, the movie star. Connor Faulkes, the leading man, the love interest, the romantic lead. Connor Faulkes, aka Prince Charming.

Georgie hadn't grown up in Oxley Crossing, so she didn't know if the rumours were true and Dawn had definitely not mentioned anything. As desperately as Georgie wanted to know everything about the actor (who she sometimes pretended was her own leading man), she knew it would be rude to ask so she kept her mouth shut. Now she was sitting in front of the house that had played out in her fantasies, wondering just what its secrets were and whether she would be lucky enough to learn any of them.

"Don't be an idiot," Georgie said to herself with a shake of her head.

She gathered together her iPad, her copy of 'A Royal Engagement', her over-large and over-flowing handbag, and the Tupperware container of freshly made muffins and bumped her hip against the door of her car to close it. Juggling everything else in her arms, she beeped her car locked and walked up the paved path. She admired the immaculately trimmed hedges and clearly delineated garden beds with their sharply trimmed edges, freshly laid mulch and not a single weed to mar the landscaping. There were three tiled steps that lead to the tiled front porch and the imposing door with a striking red Waratah beautifully represented in lead-light.

Not for the first time, Georgie wondered what she was doing here. The Bookish Book Club was normally held at Bookish, her bookshop/cafe, but somehow she had been convinced to move it to Dawn's house while she was recuperating. The other ladies hadn't minded and initially, neither had Georgie. That was until this morning when she realised she wouldn't be in the familiar surroundings of her cozy little shop. Georgie was not the adventurous type and much preferred to enjoy the wonders of the world through the pages of a book rather than in actual real life. She lived her life between her apartment in the attic above her shop, her shop, and the local grocery store. And she liked it that way.

But here she was, completely out of her comfort zone, on the steps of a relative stranger's home, bound by a commitment that she wished she'd been brave enough to refuse. That's what it came down to, really. She'd been too afraid to say no, which had forced her to do something she was even more afraid of doing. Oh why hadn't she called Dawn and told her she was sick? But that would mean using the phone, cold calling someone she'd only ever spoken to in her shop, and that was just as far out of her comfort zone as coming here was. Her irrational fear of the telephone - well, it was more about speaking on the phone, she was just fine with text messages - meant that coming here for the Book Club was the lesser of two evils.

Gah! She was making herself crazy the longer she stood in front of the door over analysing why she was here. So, girding her loins, she took a deep breath and... well, knocked. She couldn't see a door bell anywhere and she didn't have a free hand with which to knock. She used her head - literally, not figuratively - she knocked on the door. Just as she was going in for the third knock - because you always knock in threes - the door opened and instead of her head hitting the wooden door, she hit something else. Something warm and firm and distinctly male.

The shock of it caused her to stumble into him, colliding with all that maleness. She dropped everything that she had been holding in her arms in attempts to break her fall. Unprepared for her assault on his person, the man - who she still didn't know - overbalanced and the two of them landed in a heap on the gleaming wooden floor in the foyer. Her glasses slipped off her nose and skidded away, her handbag spewing its contents around them, her iPad made a suspicious cracking sound as it hit the floor and her brand new copy of 'A Royal Engagement' went skidding down the hall. Her fall was cushioned by that male body as she landed on top of him, eliciting a deep and breathless 'oof!' from him.

Mortification was the only emotion she felt as she lay there, unmoving, and hoping for the world to end. This was way beyond embarrassment. On a scale of one to ten, with one being mild blushing and ten being ground-opening-up-embarrassment, this was about forty-seven.

"Are you injured?" a deep, rich and familiar voice asked.

No, no, no. This could not get any worse, except yes, actually, it could.

"Miss?"

She opened her mouth to speak, but no words came out. No. Words. She couldn't think of a single word as she lay sprawled over the top of a body that she had a sneaking suspicion was insured in the millions. Would he sue her for reckless endangerment? How much was that going to cost her? She had no idea and a quick mental calculation of what was in her bank balance was enough for her to know that there was no way she could pay whatever the damages were.

"Connor? What was that noise?"

"It's all right Gran," he called back, his voice rumbling through his chest and into Georgie's.

The sound of Dawn's voice prompted Georgie into action and she jumped up and backed away from the man on the floor without making eye contact. She was sure she must be blushing a bright, vibrant red from the top of her blonde pigtails to the tips of her pink Converse. She cursed her English skin that seemed to telegraph her every emotion without her permission. She squinted at the floor trying to see the bright pink of her frames, but everything was a hazy, fuzzy mess. She squatted down and started feeling around the floor, hoping to find her glasses before she stepped on them, and her hand landed on something warm and thick and definitely not her glasses.

"I don't think that's what you're looking for," he said as he lifted her hand from his thigh and put her glasses in it, "But these might be."

She slid her glasses on, the world becoming clear again, and looked directly into the blue eyes of the man she had only ever seen on movie screens, in magazines, and on her computer screen. Connor Faulkes. Prince Charming.

"T-t-thank you," she managed to stutter before standing up quickly and nearly losing her balance again. She began to gather

her things without looking at him, all the time praying that she would wake up and that this would be nothing but a bad dream.

"Let me help—"

"NO!" She took a breath, "I mean, no thank you," she said, still not making eye contact. "It's fine, I've got it."

Georgie managed to gather her things together and finally stood upright, desperate to get away from the man who she'd had a very teenage-like crush on since she'd first seen him in 'The Lavender Keeper,' his first movie and also her favourite.

"I'm Connor," he said, "Dawn's grandson."

"Oh, hi. I'm Georgie," she still couldn't look at him because she knew if she did she would lose her hard-won capacity to speak. "Um, sorry about, well, that."

'Very good, Georgie,' she thought to herself, 'way to impress him with your sparkling conversational skills.'

He chuckled and the deliciousness of it skittered over her and she had to fight the desire to swoon. She was being utterly ridiculous and part of her was decidedly peeved at the way she had become a simpering mess around a man who was just a man. The other part of her reminded her that she was pretty much like this around all men. Well, all men except for her LAN party friends who she didn't think of as, well, men. Huh. That was rather mean of her. They were men, of course, just not the type of men that made her speechless and clumsy.

"I take it you're here for the Book Club?" he asked and she just nodded. "You're not hurt are you?"

"Just my pride," she said and then bit her lip to make sure nothing else inappropriate came out of her mouth. Her cheeks burned and she wished fervently for this awkward situation to be over.

He chuckled again and the reached to take the Tupperware container of mercifully undamaged muffins. "Let me take these to the kitchen and I'll show you where Gran is."

He walked away, down the hall and she followed at a safe

distance, definitely not looking at what a fine figure he cut from behind.

"Here we are," he said to her, stopping at the entrance to a large, sunny room. "Look who I found, Gran."

"Oh Georgie, dear," Dawn said from her seat on a recliner, her broken leg elevated and encased in a bright purple plaster cast.

Georgie crossed the room to drop a quick kiss on her cheek. Okay, so they weren't exactly strangers. Dawn had become a great friend and Georgie was saddened to see her laid up. The woman was always so vibrant and active and Georgie constantly forgot that she was in her seventies. She only hoped she looked that good when she reached Dawn's age.

"Connor!" Dawn called before he had a chance to leave the room. "I know that in that container are some of Georgie's famous muffins and I will know if there are any missing."

Georgie made the mistake of looking at him as he flashed his mega-watt grin at his Gran and she felt a few of her brain cells melt in the blinding rays. Oh, God, she couldn't do this. How was she supposed to facilitate an interesting and lively discussion with him here? She could barely string two intelligent words together, let alone a full sentence.

"Let me look at your shirt," Dawn said as Connor left the room with her muffins.

Georgie grinned. Her customers loved her custom made t-shirts. When she wasn't reading or playing online games, she was designing bookmarks, posters, and t-shirts with quirky sayings and obscure quotes from books and movies. Today's shirt was ironically appropriate considering the company, and also completely accidental. It was hot pink with three check boxes that said, 'Single,' 'Taken,' and 'Waiting for Prince Charming.' Of course the check box next to 'Waiting for Prince Charming' had a great big tick in it - a nod to her love of fairy tales, not the real life Prince Charming in the other room.

Dawn laughed. "I love it," she said.

There was a knock on the door and they heard Connor call out, "I'll get it."

"Sit," Dawn said, "I can't wait to get started today. I loved this book."

And so Book Club began as the rest of their rag-taggle members trooped in and took the seats. Georgie took a deep breath and put Connor Faulkes determinedly out of her mind.

2

When Connor had agreed to help his Gran host her Book Club, he expected a bunch of old ladies sitting around talking about cozy mysteries or serious biographies, not romance stories. Since coming to stay with Gran while she recuperated, he had discovered her romance book addiction and he'd been a little shocked. He knew RomComs were popular at the box office, but he didn't realise people still read them.

He was twice surprised when he discovered the book they were reading this month, a book he was well acquainted with, unbeknownst to the women in the next room. He'd had the script for months and shooting was supposed to begin in a few weeks. His presence here was actually delaying the shooting schedule, but he couldn't let Gran try to survive on her own with a broken leg. His mother was with his sister, who was expecting her first baby, and didn't want to miss the blessed event. Neither of his brothers could get away from their jobs and his father was next to useless when it came what he thought of as 'women's work.' Besides, he loved Gran and more than that, enjoyed her company. It wasn't a hardship to spend a few weeks in the country with her until she got back on her feet.

Despite the rumours, he hadn't grown up here, but he had spent a lot of time in Oxley Crossing. With both parents working, school holidays meant being shipped off to his grandparents. He much preferred Gran to his father's parents, who were a little too staid and stoic for a boy who loved adrenaline and would seek out adventures whenever left unsupervised. Gran's house and large yard in the quiet Northern Tablelands town was a safe place for him to act out all his imaginative adventures and Gran encouraged him, much to the displeasure of his parents who had high hopes of him becoming a doctor or accountant or something with a future.

Connor wanted to be a stunt man at the very least and an action hero at the most and he'd ended up somewhere in between. He'd managed to pick up a few jobs on local television and then when 'The Lavender Keeper' was being filmed right here, just a few miles from Oxley Crossing, he'd scored a job on set. When the lead actor had had a meltdown due to some insignificant detail to do with his accommodations, they'd asked Connor to step in so they could at least rehearse a few scenes and check lighting and blocking. The director had seen something in him in those very raw and unrehearsed scenes and had offered him the job after firing the other actor. And just like that, Connor had become a star.

It wasn't the fame that had attracted him, it was the chance to be someone else for a while. He liked the escape and he liked the challenge of playing a different character, although lately, they had all started to blend into one. He would dearly love to take on a meatier role, something with more depth and a bit of action, or even do a stint behind the camera as a director, but for now he was type cast as the romantic lead. He'd made a commitment to this next movie and then he was going to take a break and find something that reignited the passion that had been lacking from his last few roles. He was a big enough star and made enough money to be choosey with his next role and he'd been working diligently to get to this point, so why not take the time and choose something he really wanted to do?

He heard the group laugh and the soft chuckle of Georgie made his ears prick up. She had been the biggest surprise of all. When he thought of 'Book Club', he did not think of a cute little blonde in pig tails with big blue eyes and converse shoes wrapped up in skinny jean shorts and a bright pink t-shirt. If anything he expected a matronly librarian type or a septuagenarian like his grandmother. She also didn't seem to recognise him which, despite being a hit to his ego, was refreshing. He knew that with fame came fans and he appreciated them, but it was nice to be normal for once and not on his guard for some misguided young woman who might throw herself at him. He didn't think he would ever walk into his room here at Gran's and find Georgie waiting for him with more than conversation on her mind. It sounded conceited to even think about such a situation, but unfortunately it had happened to him on a few occasions when his hotel location had been leaked. After the fourth time, he demanded more security. Not that he was afraid for his safety, but he did not want to wake up to pictures of himself sleeping splashed all over social media. The paparazzi was bad enough without adding the rabid fans to the mix.

"Connor," Gran called, "Come and meet the ladies and bring those muffins of Georgie's."

Connor smiled as he plated up the muffins and flicked on the kettle. No doubt the ladies would like a cup of tea with their muffins and the least he could do was play host for Gran. He took the muffins into the airy sitting room, his PR smile on his face.

"Ladies," he said, winking at Gran.

The group of women looked back at him, their eyes wide, all except Georgie who seemed more interested in the loose thread on her jeans than him.

"You're Connor Faulkes," one of the women said, awe in her voice.

"Yes ma'am," he replied.

"No, I mean, you are *the* Connor Faulkes. Prince Charming."

His grin turned wry. He'd done three back to back movies, a trilogy, in which he played the fairy tale prince bought to life by a bunch of teenage geek girls and their computer. They had become his highest grossing films, popular with both teenagers and adults alike.

"Don't gush over him," Gran said, "His head is already filled with enough of that crap from his agent and all those breathless fans that follow him around."

Trust his grandmother to keep it real, but he wasn't upset. He liked that she was the one to make sure the fame didn't change him.

"She's right," he said, "While I'm here, I'm just plain old Connor, Dawn Hawkes' grandson. Now, would you ladies like tea or coffee?"

WHILE THE LADIES gave their drink orders to Connor, Georgie took particular interest in her iPad, which had indeed cracked when it hit the shiny, wooden floor in the foyer. It was not the first time something like that had happened and it probably wouldn't be the last. Georgie carried her iPad everywhere with her, it was an extension of herself, and being as clumsy as she was it was inevitable that she dropped it often. Even with a case on it, she'd managed to crack the screen several times and was grateful that one of her LAN party buddies knew how to fix them. Of all the times she'd dropped it though, this was the most embarrassing. Even the time she knocked it off the bathroom sink in her ensuite while she was on the loo wasn't as embarrassing as what had happened earlier.

"Georgie?"

That voice. Oh God, that voice saying her name. Her brain froze as their eyes met and she felt like a blubbering idiot, but was incapable to do or say anything under his hypnotic gaze.

"Tea, coffee, Bonox?"

The room tittered with the old joke, but Georgie just swallowed thickly.

"Ah, water," she croaked, "Please," she added hurriedly as an afterthought.

Connor winked at her and turned to leave. Did he really wink at her? Oh God he winked at her and now all the ladies of Book Club were looking at her. She cleared her throat, trying to think of something, anything, to say to get the attention off her and her stupid inability to be able to behave like a normal human being in the presence of a man.

"So, the book. What did everyone think?"

Georgie barely listened to the comments as she tried to corral her thoughts into something resembling intelligence. Her stern part gave her simpering part a talking to, reminding said simpering part that Connor was a mere mortal and just as fallible as any other mere mortal. Both agreed that he was the most delectable mere mortal they had ever had the privilege to lay eyes on. With the two of them discussing him and bickering over him, Georgie could barely keep herself from running from the house in a fit of crazy. With a good bit of hard won self-control, she managed to shut up the voices in her head and refocus on the discussion.

The book they were reading, or had read, wasn't anything too deep but it did discuss some issues relating to women in authority and the ongoing glass ceiling that a lot of women still faced as they rose up the ranks in their chosen career. Of course this was told in a whimsical tale of an imaginary country with an imaginary Royal family. Despite the fairytale-esque setting, it still managed to convey the struggle of a young modern woman thrust into a politically unstable environment where the 'Boy's Club' was still very much in power. And it was a romance, which was the whole point. The Bookish Book Club was all about romance, the members being fiercely loyal to the genre and not afraid to admit it.

"I liked the parallels to Pride and Prejudice," Dawn said, capturing Georgie's attention.

"How so?" she asked.

"Well, Lord Darkly is most definitely based on Mr. Darcy, don't you think?"

"Oh, yes," Maureen chimed in, "I didn't see it at first, but I do now. The way he is so gruff with her at first and so disapproving of her association with Jordan."

Maureen was a lovely fifty-ish woman who looked more like seventy. She was all grey hair and blue rinse with a tight perm and thick glasses. Georgie thought perhaps she was trying too hard to fit in with the septuagenerian crowd and she was a Dawn devotee, agreeing with nearly everything the other woman said.

"That's the only similarity, though," Georgie interjected, "I mean, the story itself isn't anything like Pride and Prejudice."

"No, I suppose not," Dawn agreed, thoughtfully and Maureen doggedly nodded along too.

"And Will had every right to be upset with her for associating with Jordan," Kendra said, "After all, he wasn't very nice in the end."

Kendra was the only other person in the room the same age as Georgie and they were best friends. Kendra worked on her parents' sheep station on the outskirts of town and when she was working she wore the uniform of the bush - jeans and a flannelette shirt with boots and an Akubra. When she wasn't on the farm, Kendra was all woman. Pretty dresses and high heels, makeup and her dark hair glossy and styled. If Connor was going to wink at anyone, then it should be Kendra, not her.

"Here we are, ladies," Connor said returning to the room with a tray of cups.

Georgie couldn't look away as his biceps flexed, stretching the sleeve of his t-shirt, when he lowered the tray to the coffee table in the centre of the circle of chairs. He plucked a dainty teacup and saucer from the tray and handed it to Dawn, followed by handing out the rest of the cups to each person. The women smiled and blushed prettily as he gave them attention, remembering their names and their beverage requests. He saved Georgie for last, but it still wasn't enough time for her to get her hormones under control and as he handed her the glass of ice water, the ice cubes clinking merrily against the rim. Her hand shook so much that she ended up dumping the whole lot in her lap.

Georgie jumped up with a squeal to a chorus of gasps from the assembled women. Her crotch was saturated with water cold enough to give her frostbite and rivulets of water ran down her bare legs and pooled in her Converse high tops. She saw the twitch of his lips as he tried not to laugh and flushed with embarrassment as she realised he was looking at the wet patch on her shorts. His eyes flicked up to hers, not worried in the least that he had been ogling her, and he grinned, his dimples blinding her and making her forget momentarily that she was embarrassed and mad at him.

"Oh, Georgie," Dawn said, trying to get out of her chair to help, "Are you okay?"

"She's fine, Gran," Connor said, "You stay where you are. I'll help Georgie clean up."

"NO!" Georgie took a breath and said more calmly, "It's fine, it's only water. But if I could get a towel?"

Connor grabbed her hand and tugged her towards the door of the room, "Come on, I'll show you where the bathroom is."

The heat of his hand on her arm burned a trail through her body, warming her from the inside out and she followed him, numbly. He really should come with a warning label.

❧ 3 ❧

The events of Book Club stayed with Georgie for the rest of the week and by Saturday, Book Club being on Wednesday, she expected the burning humiliation to have been just a distant memory. Unfortunately, when she saw Connor's large frame walk through the door of her shop, it all came rushing back over her like an avalanche and she headed for the stacks in the back so she wouldn't have to face him. Thankfully Millie, her part-time employee and second best friend, was manning the front counter. Georgie couldn't help but watch him, though, from her hiding place, curious to know why he was even gracing her store with his movie-star presence.

"Hi, welcome to Bookish," Millie said brightly.

She knew all about the incident at Book Club, thanks to the gossiping mouths of Kendra and several of the other ladies that had been present. By now half the town knew of her humiliation and nearly everyone had given her that knowing look when they'd come in for their daily caffeine fix.

"Uh, hi," Connor said, his very masculine voice at odds with the very feminine atmosphere Georgie had created inside Bookish. "My Gran sent me down to pick up some books?" He sounded so unsure that Georgie had to smile. The one thing she had never imagined was Connor Faulkes being less than alpha male confident in everything he did.

"Okay," Millie said, drawing the word out, and Georgie knew she was puzzled.

It was at that moment that she realised she hadn't given anyone the list of books that Dawn had requested and she was the only one who knew why Connor was here.

"Shoot," she cursed under her breath. She was going to have to face him after all.

She took a breath and banged her head on the shelf a couple of times before working up the courage to go out there and do her job. She just had to think of him as just another customer, not the man who starred in her dreams at night, or the man she had made a complete fool of herself in front of, not once, but twice. She could do this. She could.

"It's all right, Millie," she called, taking a step from behind the shelf where she had been hiding, "I have Dawn's list."

He looked up and saw her then, their eyes meeting across the rows of books, the smell of old books and new in the atmosphere, the sunlight dancing through the front windows and gathering around him like a halo. She took a step towards him, her foot connecting with a pile of second hand books she had yet to shelve, and with the elegance of a newborn giraffe still trying to find its legs, she sprawled across the floor, landing at his feet. How many more times was she going to humiliate herself in front of him? Surely three times was the charm?

"You really need to stop falling for me," he said as he squatted down in front of her.

She banged her head on the floor a couple of times before pushing herself up and onto her backside, giving up any pretence of gracefulness or even normal human behaviour, and leant against the bookshelf at her back. He sat beside her in companionable silence, but he didn't have to speak to have her body in a tizzy and her mind a mush of garbled rubbish, just his closeness was enough.

"You must think I'm a complete fool," she said, her voice flat and monotone.

"Not at all," he said, bumping shoulders with her, "I think you're cute."

"Cute? Isn't that something you say about a kitten that gets themselves all tangled up in a ball of wool?"

"I suppose that would be cute too," he said with a nod, "But I like the way you get all tongue-tied and clumsy around me."

Georgie dropped her head in her hands and moaned. "That's the only way you've ever seen me," she whined.

"Not true," he said, "I listened in to your Book Club. You had some well thought out things to say."

"Which makes my performance whenever you're around so completely obvious. I say again, you must think I am a complete fool."

"Nah. I'm flattered, actually. I've never had that effect on anyone before."

Georgie snorted and then gasped in horror which only made him laugh.

"Surely I am not the first woman that you've left in a snivelling heap?"

"I have to say that of all my interactions with women, none have even come close to those I've had with you."

"Oh God," she moaned, her face blazing, "Kill me now."

He chuckled and stood, holding out a hand to her.

"Come on," he said, "I need to get these books for Gran or she won't let me go out to play this afternoon."

Georgie let him help her up and then set about finding the books Dawn had ordered.

"What big plans do you have this afternoon that you can't miss?"

"Rock climbing."

Georgie looked at him with horror. "Rock climbing? Are you insane?"

He laughed, a big booming sound that filled the shop and made everything seem to smile around her.

"I'm going out to Wollomombi Falls with this group of outdoor adventurers. We're camping there tonight so we can get an early start on the climb in the morning. You should come."

"Me? Rock climbing? Have you seen me trying to walk on flat ground?"

He laughed again and it was a sound that Georgie now ranked as her favourite among all the sounds in the world.

"I could teach you."

"Yeah, not going to happen." She piled a load of books into his arms. "I like to do my adventuring through the pages of a book from the comfort of my overstuffed couch with a warm blanket and a cup of tea."

He smiled at her, his dimples winking and whispering secret things to her that she refused to listen to. "It would be fun."

"Yeah for everybody else as they stand around laughing at me as I plunge to my death from the rocky outcropping."

Connor leaned in close and she could smell the woodsy scent of his aftershave and the musky smell of his maleness. "I would never let you fall," he whispered before walking toward the counter with the books for Dawn.

She stood rooted to the spot, unable to move for fear of rushing after him and plastering herself against him, begging him to take her with him. He paid for his purchases and waved to her as he walked out the door, leaving her behind thinking that maybe it wouldn't be so bad to fall off the side a mountain if it meant she got to spend a little bit more time with him.

"It really is him," Millie said.

"Hmmm?"

"Connor Faulkes. That really was him and he really is Dawn's grandson."

"Yes," Georgie replied, shelving the books that she tripped over earlier.

"I don't think I really believed Kendra when she told me, but I can't deny it now."

"Didn't you grow up here? Didn't you already know he was Dawn's grandson?"

Millie shook her head. "I moved here in high school and we spent summers at the beach. If I'd known he was going to be here during the holidays, I would have gladly given up my bikinis and tan."

"So he didn't grow up here?"

"Not according to Kendra. She remembers him. He used to only come during school holidays and he's a couple years older than us. I think by the time I moved here, he didn't visit so much anymore."

"Well as far as I'm concerned, he can stop visiting."

"Oh come on, you don't really mean that."

"No, actually, I do. I'm an utter moron whenever he's around. The sooner he goes back to where ever he came from, the sooner I can get back to being a normal person."

Millie laughed. "I don't think he minds your quirks."

Georgie lifted her eyebrows at Millie's comment. "What makes you say that?"

"He seemed to like you. He even sat on the floor with you while you whined."

Georgie's face flushed again and she covered it with her hands. "See what I mean! Moron!"

"Oh honey, I really don't think he sees you that way. God, if he looked at me the way he looks at you I'd be all over him."

"At least you don't turn into a blubbering idiot whenever he's around."

"It's just your lack of experience, that's all."

"How am I supposed to become experienced when I can't be around a normal guy without losing fifty IQ points and my ability to put sentences together?"

"That's it!" Millie exclaimed.

"What's it?"

"Exposure therapy."

"I don't like the sound of that."

"No, it's perfect," Millie said, warming to the subject. "I was reading an article on it and how they use it to help people overcome anxieties and fears."

"I don't have a man phobia," Georgie huffed.

"No, but you do get all tied up in knots around men and it's only because you didn't have the normal socialisation around the opposite sex that Kendra and I did."

"I went to an all-girl school. You make it sound like I was raised in a nunnery."

"Well you may as well have been. Did you even date?"

"I've been on a date," Georgie said softly.

"How many dates?"

Georgie mumbled her answer into the shelves.

"One date?" Millie yelled, appalled.

"A little louder. I don't think the ladies at the CWA knitting circle heard you."

"Are you serious?" Millie asked in a furious whisper coming to huddle beside her in the stacks.

Georgie shrugged, not looking at Millie. "I don't know if you would even call it a date, really," she said, "I was helping a guy study and we had pizza."

Millie slapped herself in the forehead. "Oh my God! Georgie this is not okay."

"I think it's perfectly okay."

"No. No it is not. How are you ever meant to meet Prince Charming if you never date?"

"I meet Prince Charming all the time," Georgie replied, "I've had lots of book boyfriends and been in love multiple times."

"But they're not real!"

"And that's the best part," Georgie said becoming exasperated with the conversation. "I don't have to try and be perfect, I don't have to think of things to say. I don't trip over or fall on my butt. My hair is always perfect and I never have to worry about having my heart broken."

"Are you telling me you would rather spend your life with your nose buried in a book living vicariously through fictional characters instead of getting out there and meeting a real guy and having a real kiss?"

Georgie looked Millie in the eye. "Yes," she said simply and, quite honestly, it was exactly what she expected her life to look like.

CONNOR STOWED his gear in the back of his shiny new truck and climbed into the cab. He couldn't remember ever feeling so amped up for a camping trip and it had been far too long since he'd indulged in a little bit of adventure. The fact that he hadn't stopped smiling since he left Bookish meant nothing, although seeing Georgie trip and fall had been funny - in a Funniest Home Videos kind of way, not a mean kind of way. Her clumsiness delighted him in a way he never thought clumsiness could. She wasn't even trying to be charming or cute, she just was and it warmed something in him.

He drove away from Gran's house, pointing the truck in the direction of the campsite. He'd organised some home care to help Gran for the night and tomorrow, although she had scolded him and told him it was unnecessary. He felt an obligation to her though and didn't want anything to happen to her while he was out of cell phone range. He knew that if the campsite wasn't out of range, the mountain definitely would be.

His fingers practically itched to feel the rough stone beneath them. He had been working so much lately that it had been an age since he'd gotten any time to indulge his hobbies. He also knew that if his agent knew he was about to go rock climbing, he would have an apoplexy. It was dangerous and he wouldn't deny that, but he also wasn't stupid. He only climbed with other people and he always took care. He liked the adrenalin rush of climbing, but he didn't want to die doing it.

Georgie's face when he had invited her to join him had been hilarious. The abject horror that filled her eyes was so genuine that it had shocked him into laughter. She did have a point though. She could barely keep upright on flat ground; putting her on the side of a mountain was a recipe for disaster. It made him wonder if it was just him or whether all men made her act like that. He didn't think for a minute that she was putting it on to get attention, but it did make him wonder about how much experience she had with men.

Thinking of her with other men made him clench his hands on the steering wheel. What the hell? He barely knew her so he shouldn't be feeling jealous. Her social life was none of his concern and he shouldn't even be speculating about it. Besides, she wasn't his type anyway. She was cute with her jeans and quirky t-shirts - today's was bright purple with a large pair of glasses on it and the words 'talk nerdy to me' - but she wasn't the kind of woman he normally dated. And she was too short. He was six four and she barely came up to his chin, and what the hell was with her hair? Twice now he'd seen her; the first time she'd worn it in pigtails like a five year old and this time it was in two buns at the sides of her head. She also seemed to have an attachment to Converse sneakers, which he could appreciate, but he thought weird on a full grown woman. None of his girlfriends had ever worn Converse, they wore heels unless they were going to the gym and then it was whatever the latest and greatest pair of athletic shoes was the flavour of the month. And another thing, she colour coordinated her glasses to her t-shirts...okay, well, he had only seen her twice, but both times the colour of her frames matched the colour of her shirt. How many pairs of glasses did the woman have?

No. Georgie was not his type at all. The press would have a field day if he took her on a date. They would rip her to shreds in a heartbeat and he just wouldn't do that to her. She was nice and friendly and adorable. She was also way too soft to battle with the paparazzi so it was a good thing that she wasn't his type anyway. She would never have to worry about the paps hunting her every step like they did with him.

"Gran," Connor warned, but she didn't listen to him.

"Everyone," Dawn said to the ladies when they had taken their seats. "Connor is going to be joining us for Book Club."

He watched Georgie's eyes go wide as the implications settled in. He would be in the room and so far she had hardly been able to string two words together whenever he was around. Maybe this was a good thing, maybe she would finally relax around him and they could actually have a conversation that didn't involve slapstick comedy.

"Um," Georgie began, stopping to clear her throat and take a sip of water. "Has he read the material?" She deliberately wouldn't meet his eyes and it annoyed him. He thought they'd at least started to get past the awkwardness after what happened at her shop.

"I have," he said.

"In fact," Dawn said, her voice turning conspiratorial, "He is going to be in the upcoming movie."

A round of gasps greeted her announcement and Connor had to be really careful not to roll his eyes.

"They're making a movie of 'A Royal Engagement'?" Georgie asked.

Dawn nodded.

"They're planning on making the whole series," Connor said, "But that will depend on how the first one goes."

"So, you see, Connor needs to be in the Book Club so he can get a feel for the character."

"Which, um, which character?"

Georgie actually looked at him that time when she asked the question and he felt irrationally pleased.

"Will Darkly," he replied.

The women gathered all nodded sagely like it was of course the only role he could and should play. He had asked his agent to petition for the role of Jordan Wicks, but casting wouldn't have a bar of it. They wanted him for Darkly and that's what he got. It wasn't that he didn't want the role, he was just sick of playing the same character over and over again. Although he had to admit, Darkly did have a darker, broody side that was a little different for him.

"So have you read the book or just the script?" Georgie asked.

"Just the script," he admitted sheepishly.

With an adorably cute smirk, Georgie pointed to her t-shirt. It was a pale blue today (yes, her glasses matched) and written on the front was 'Don't judge a book by its movie'.

"Ha," he said, genuinely delighted.

"But he does have a general idea," Dawn insisted, "And I'll make sure he reads the book before next week."

Georgie smiled, "It's okay Dawn. It's fine for Connor to join Book Club, we don't have an exclusivity policy, and everybody is welcome. The only thing I ask is that everyone read the book and that we are respectful of each other's opinions. Books are subjective; different people see different things in a book, sometimes even different from what the author intended." She looked at each of the members, "So that means no one try and influence

Connor in his opinion of the character. He needs to find it for himself and it is the only way he will be able to play Darkly authentically."

Connor was floored by her little speech and really grateful for it. The last thing he wanted was everyone's opinions shoved down his throat. She was exactly right in what she said; he needed to find the character's voice himself, which was one of the reasons he didn't want to do this whole Book Club thing. Now that he was here, maybe he could glean something from it. It would be interesting to see how other people viewed his character and the way he interacted with the other characters in the book.

"Thank you Georgie," he said, smiling at her, a genuine smile which got wider when she flushed bright red. It really shouldn't make him happy to make her blush, but he enjoyed it maybe a little too much.

She reached for her water and nearly knocked it over, saving it at the last minute, then took a sip before clearing her throat and turning to the rest of the group.

"Okay, let's get started."

Connor was impressed with the discussion that flowed around him. The book was a romance and he had only ever taken the story at face value, but these women looked beyond the words written to the themes that ran through the book. He had to admit that the script lacked a lot of the undertones that the book seemed to portray, but that was where character came into it. He also had a bit more insight into the Will Darkly character than they did. The book was written entirely from Alyssa's point of view, but the script had some scenes from Will's point of view which threw a whole different light on his behaviour. He was in two minds as to whether to share what was on his mind.

"Connor," Georgie said, addressing him directly which was enough to break into his thoughts, "You look like you have something to say."

"I didn't know whether or not to share something that I know from the script that doesn't appear in the book."

The women all seemed to lean forward towards him, eager to hear what he had to say.

"Is it relevant to the discussion?" Georgie asked, a smile playing around her lips.

"It's about Will and his reasons for doing what he does."

Georgie looked around at the faces of the women who were all trained on him and smiled at him. "I think we all want to hear."

"The script has some scenes from Will's point of view, which I don't think are in the book. It shows the reason why he acts so coolly towards Alyssa."

"The end of the book sort of explains that," Georgie said, "Do you think having those scenes earlier in the film dilutes the narrative?"

His eyes widened, not having thought about it like that... and not really knowing the answer. "I think I would have to read the book before I could comment on that," he said.

"What do you ladies think?" she asked, "If we were to see Will's motives and Jordan's duplicity before the climax at the end, would it ruin the story?"

Connor smiled to himself, he liked this more assertive side of Georgie. She seemed to have gotten over her awkwardness now that Book Club was well under way. He was finally getting to see the real Georgie, which wasn't all that different really, except she could actually string intelligent sentences together. He already knew she was capable of such after eavesdropping on their meeting last week. He was just glad that now she could do it while he was in the room.

"I DON'T KNOW ABOUT THIS," Georgie said as the stood on the sidewalk in front of the local bar.

The music was loud, the crowd inside was even louder, and

Georgie felt completely out of her element. Aside from the fact that she wasn't a big drinker, had never stepped foot inside the local pub and didn't know how to dance, Kendra and Millie had dressed her and done her hair and makeup and she felt like an absolute fraud. No one would believe she was a cool chick. She could barely walk in the three inch heels that Kendra had forced on her feet and the skirt she wore was so short that she kept pulling it down in the hopes that it would cover a bit more leg. Even her boobs felt wrong. They were plumped up from a push-up bra and they felt like they were choking her. At least the v-neck of her top showed off her cleavage because she would hate to have gone through all that torture for her still to be as flat as a pancake.

The big reveal in her bedroom mirror had left her gob smacked and disbelieving her own eyes. The only thing she recognised was her black cat's eye glasses with the shiny rhinestones on the corners. Everything else was alien to her. Her blonde hair had been washed, blow dried and straightened and now hung down her back in a long sheet of shimmering gold. Who knew her hair could look like that? Millie had slapped enough makeup on her to plug the holes in the Dutch dike. Her eyes looked big and blue and exotic with their long dark lashes, and the liquid liner that kicked up at the edges giving them more of an almond shape. Millie and Kendra had debated heatedly over what colour lipstick to use, but eventually settled on red. But not just red... Vamp Red, a colour she had never even heard of before. Whoever the girl had been looking back at her from the mirror definitely wasn't her.

"Come on," Millie said, hooking her elbow through Georgie's. "Just pretend for one night that you actually have a social life."

"I have a social life," Georgie replied.

"A social life that actually means leaving your apartment?"

"I go to parties—"

Kendra snorted. "LAN parties are not parties," she said with the authority of someone who had a social life. "Come on, it's one night. Have one drink with us, one dance and if you absolutely hate it, we'll let you go home."

Georgie bit the corner of her lip, trying hard not to mess up the lipstick and get it all over her teeth, because that is something that would definitely happen to her, before nodding.

"Okay, one drink."

"And one dance," Millie reminded her.

"Fine. One drink and one dance."

"Whoo hoo!" they both chorused as they dragged Georgie up the stairs and into the pub.

It was dark inside and smoky and the music was so loud that the bass line made her chest vibrate. The coloured lights pulsed and the crush of people was a little claustrophobic. All of it combined made her want to head for the nearest exit, but her two so-called friends had a strong grip on her arms and she had no hope of escape. If someone had asked her what her idea of hell was, she was pretty sure that this would be it. This exact thing. And yet here she was, voluntarily entering the lion's den.

The girls pulled her through the crowd and up to the bar where Millie ordered them three shots of tequila.

"So this is my one drink, right?" Georgie yelled over the noise.

"God, no," Millie replied, "This is just the warm up. Shots don't count."

Kendra showed her how to lick, sip and suck and she tossed the shot back with a grimace, thankful for the lime to suck on to remove the vile taste from her mouth.

"That was awful!" she said, but no one was listening to her. Millie was ordering a pitcher of margaritas and Kendra was looking for a table.

"Look! Over here!" Kendra yelled and then started dragging her through the crush.

Georgie fell gratefully into the newly vacated seat as Millie put the pitcher in the middle of the table along with three glasses rimmed with salt. Kendra splashed the icy cold liquid into each glass and then lifted hers for a toast.

"Here's to finding Georgie a social life!"

"Hey!" Georgie protested.

They clinked glasses and drank. The fresh, crisp citrus taste with a hit of salt buzzed over Georgie's tongue and she licked her lips in bliss.

"Wow," she said, "I really like that."

"Then drink up, girlfriend!" Millie said, topping up her glass.

Georgie took another big gulp, giving herself a brain freeze which made her whine and giggle at the same time. Her knees felt fizzy, like the blood was bubbling through her veins and her body felt warm. She knew her cheeks must have been flushed, but she didn't care. Her mind was loose and she felt giddy, not in a bad way, but in a 'let's party' kind of way.

How long had it been since she'd let her hair down - figuratively and literally? Moving to Oxley Crossing, setting up her shop, and getting Book Club off the ground seemed to swallow all her time. She loved what she did, she loved her shop and Book Club and her little apartment, but they were all time sucks and she was left feeling like she was always busy but with little to show for it. She had never been very much of a party girl, but before coming here she'd at least had a social life, hadn't she?

"Finish your drink," Millie said as she filled Georgie's glass once more, "And then we'll hit the dance floor."

Georgie drank her margarita down, swallowing the whole thing and then she jumped to her feet, swaying a little bit on the unfamiliar stilettos.

"Let's dance!" she cried, shooting both hands in the air like a prize fighter. The girls yahoo-ed as they followed her through the crowd to the small patch of floor that was designated for dancing. Georgie shook her hips and shimmied to the beat and wondered why she hadn't done this sooner.

. . .

THE FIRST THING he noticed was that she couldn't dance... but she was enthusiastic. He couldn't put his finger on just what was wrong with what she was doing except that it looked wrong, awkward, and a little off beat.

The second thing he noticed was her golden hair that shimmied under the lights as she shook her booty, a booty that was barely covered. Then his eyes dropped to her legs. She wasn't tall, but she had a mile of bare leg on display and he couldn't help but appreciate them as she moved to her own music, which seemed to be nothing like the music playing through the speakers.

When she turned around it took Connor a moment to place her. She looked familiar and she was pretty darn gorgeous, so it was unusual for him to not remember her. It was her eyes in the end that got him and when he recognised Georgie he nearly choked on his beer. That was not the same woman who had been sitting in his Gran's sitting room only a couple of days ago. Who else could it be unless she had a twin?

He watched her with her friends, a smile on his face. She might not be able to dance, but she was having a hell of a time anyway. So much so that her unfettered joy was contagious and she had nearly every guy's eye in the bar on her. His grip tightened around the neck of his beer bottle as he watched the other men on the dance floor ogle her. One even had the audacity to sidle up to her and start dancing with her. She seemed a little flummoxed at his attentions, but she didn't push him away and a knot formed in his gut.

Before he knew what he was doing, he'd put down his empty bottle and was heading towards the dance floor, Georgie in his sights. He moved in close behind her and moved the gold sheet of her hair to the side so he could talk in her ear.

"Hey kitten," he said.

She jumped and then looked over her shoulder at him, her face spreading into a big grin when she saw him.

"Connor!" she said loudly over the music and threw her arms around his neck.

It was at that point that he realised she was drunk because there was no way sober Georgie would do something so forward. She was usually so discombobulated by him that she was a mess of nerves and awkwardness.

"Hey Georgie," he said, resting his hands on her hips and trying to get her to follow the rhythm of the music. He wasn't Fred Astaire, but he knew how to hold his own on the dance floor, at least a bit better than her.

"What are you doing here?" he asked when he had managed to wrangle her into some semblance of dancing.

"My home girls dragged me here," she drawled indicating Kendra from the Book Club and Millie from Bookish who had found partners of their own.

"You been drinking?"

She held her index finger and her thumb an inch or so apart and said, "Little bit."

Unless she was a super lightweight, he imagined that it was quite a bit more than a little bit.

"How about we get you something to eat?"

He tried to lead her off the dance floor but she held her ground and pouted at him.

"I wanna dance," she said, her big blue eyes pleading with him.

He sighed and stepped back into her embrace.

"Okay," he said, "One more song but you have to promise me we'll get something to eat afterwards."

"'kay," she said, winding her arms around his neck and resting her head on his chest.

He let his arms curl around her and held her close, breathing in the fruity scent of her hair. Because of her heels she fit under his chin so he could rest in on top of her head. He couldn't deny that they felt good together, like their bodies fit. Thankfully the song was a slow one and while he had her in his arms he allowed himself to relax and enjoy the feel of her pressed against him. He didn't think this would be a repeated opportunity, not with her nervousness around him. Again he wondered if it was just him or whether it was all men.

"You smell nice," she breathed against him and he had to smile.

"So do you, kitten," he replied.

She tipped her glazed eyes up to him, a puzzled expression on her face.

"It's Georgie," she said, "I'm Georgie."

"I know, kitten."

"So why do you keep calling me kitten?"

"Remember the other day when I was in your shop and I said you were cute?"

Her brow furrowed as thought and then nodded slowly.

"Do you remember what you said to me?"

"I told you cute was something you called a kitten."

"Right," he said and she grinned.

"You still think I'm cute?"

"I think you're adorable."

"Even with my Vamp Red lipstick?"

"Even with your lipstick."

She pouted then and he wanted to dip his head and kiss those Vamp Red lips.

"I was kind of going for bombshell, not cute," she said, "I guess I can't even do that right."

"Oh honey," he said, holding her tighter, "You are definitely a bombshell tonight, although I think I prefer my cute kitten Georgie."

She bit her lip and he bit back a groan. "Yeah?" she asked.

"Yeah," he whispered as the song ended. He took a breath and stepped back, loathe to let her go but knowing she needed to eat to soak up some of that alcohol in her system. "Hungry?"

"Starved," she replied.

He started to lead her through the crowd, but she pulled him in another direction.

"We have a table over here," she said in explanation.

He let her lead and then seated himself beside her, close enough that she dropped her head on his shoulder.

"I'm tired," she said, her eyes drooping.

"Eat first and then you can sleep."

"'kay," she said and snuggled against him.

He grit his teeth against the need to pull her on his lap and hold her as she fell asleep in his arms. He needed to get some food and lots and lots of water into her. He reminded himself over and over again that she wasn't his type and that he wasn't attracted to her even as she seemed to burrow into him just like a kitten might. He lifted his free hand to snag a waitress and ordered all the greasy food he could and a pitcher of ice water.

❧ 5 ☙

Georgie woke up wondering what on earth had happened the night before. She still wore the clothes she went out in, her hair was a tangled mess and her eyes felt like they were stuck together with glue. Plus there was the pounding headache and the urge to expel all the contents of her stomach. She ran for the bathroom and did just that, wondering if she was dying and whether she should call the ambulance.

Fortunately, with her stomach now empty, she felt marginally better. She pulled herself up and stripped before stepping into the shower and letting the hot water do its thing. There was something very magical and restorative about hot showers and Georgie gave thanks to the universe for their invention.

When the water began to cool, she turned off the taps and dragged herself out of the shower, wrapping her wet hair in a fluffy towel and pulling on her terry cloth robe, feeling slightly more human but grateful that it was Sunday and her shop was closed. She padded back into her bedroom and spied a glass of water on her nightstand with two pills and a note.

Sitting on the edge of her bed she read the note:

Take these and make sure you drink the whole glass of water - C

Had she slipped down the rabbit hole and found herself in wonderland? And who was 'C'?

She examined the pills and determined they were ibuprofen, so she took them as suggested and swallowed the whole glass of water. Her stomach growled, reminding her that it was now empty, so she shuffled out to her tiny kitchen, trying not to disturb her pounding head too much.

Another note was waiting for her on the sink.

Drink another glass of water before you have your coffee - C

Feeling a little weird to be following the advice of a mysterious note maker, she drank another glass of water while she waited for the kettle to boil. She didn't drink instant coffee or percolated coffee, so she made herself a cup of tea instead. Turning to the fridge for some milk she saw yet another note.

Greasy food will make you feel better. Eggs, bacon, hash brown, mushrooms... if you're up to it, meet me at The Cow and Anchor at 8am for a full English breakfast - C

Angie looked at the time. It was a quarter to eight, if she rushed, she could make it to the English pub by a little after eight. But did she want to? Did she even know a 'C' and if she did, did she want to see him or her again? How much of a fool had she made of herself last night? She had obviously been drunk enough to let this 'C' person bring her home and allow them into her apartment. Nothing untoward had happened, but it could have, which scared her a bit. Was she so drunk that she went home with a perfect stranger?

She sat down at her kitchen bench with her tea and tried to remember what happened. She remembered walking into the pub, she remembered drinking a shot and then margaritas and she remembered dancing. The rest was a bit fuzzy, but somewhere in the mix, she remembered Connor. She dropped her head to the table and banged it once and winced as her head pounded with the action. Serves her right for being so irresponsible. Had she really danced with Connor? Had she really thrown her arms around him and rested her cheek on his hard chest? Was he the mysterious 'C' that had brought her home and left her all these cute little notes?

There was only one way to find out. She drank the rest of her tea, scolding her mouth in the process and then raced to dress. She brushed her teeth and piled her hair on top of her head in a messy bun that wasn't too tight in respect for her still tender head. She grabbed her bag and her keys and headed out the door, feeling a bounce in her step despite the hangover. The bright sun pierced her eyes and she fumbled in her bag for her sunglasses, then slid into her car and pointed it in the direction of the Cow and Anchor.

CONNOR SAT in the booth of the dimly lit English pub and wondered if Georgie was even awake yet. Maybe he should have said nine? But then if he did that, by the time they ate it would be too late for the rest of what he planned for the day. He only hoped Georgie was up for it.

The big door of the pub opened and he looked up, but it wasn't her. He checked his watch, it was only just after eight, so they still had plenty of time, but he felt irrationally nervous. She might not even come. She might have been so freaked out by finding those notes that she'd think he was a stalker. Or she might not have seen his notes at all, she could very well still be asleep and he would be left sitting here like an idiot.

"Hey."

He looked up and grinned. She came. He was flushed with pleasure at seeing her, although she did look a bit worse for wear. Her eyes were red rimmed and dark smudges sat underneath them. She wore no makeup today and all that glorious golden hair was still wet from her shower and pulled up in some sort of mess on top of her head. She was back in her jean shorts and t-shirt, which said 'You read my t-shirt, that's enough socialising for the day'.

"Hey yourself," he said as she slid into the booth and put her head on the table.

"Just how much of a fool did I make of myself last night?" she mumbled, not lifting her head.

"Well, there was the dancing on the table bit—" she groaned and mumbled something unintelligible, "—then there was the buying a round of drinks for everyone in the pub—" another groan, although it could have been a whimper, "and then last but not least, your karaoke performance."

This last statement made her raise her head and look at him with mouth agape and eyes wide.

"Please tell me that's a joke," she pleaded, and he laughed.

"Had you worried, didn't I?"

"Cruel," she mumbled putting her head back down on the table, "You, sir, are a cruel, cruel man."

He laughed again, inordinately pleased with himself and with her company.

"It's okay Georgie, none of it is true and you didn't make a fool of yourself in the slightest, although I must say, drunk Georgie is far less clumsy around me than sober Georgie."

She groaned something that sounded like 'I hate you' but he just smiled. She was fun to tease.

A waitress approached and he ordered for both of them. After she left, Georgie raised her head.

"There's no way I can eat all of that," she said.

He shrugged, "Eat what you can, you're going to need it for what I have planned for today."

She sat back in her seat and looked at him sceptically.

"I have plans for today," she said.

"Not anymore you don't."

"I can't just drop everything because you want me to."

"I know what your plans were, Georgie, you told me last night.

You had a big day planned of doing laundry and finishing off the book you're reading and then you were going to tackle the fun task of sorting out your lost sock basket to try and find mates for all your single socks."

He watched as her cheeks pinked and her eyes dropped to the table.

"Have breakfast with me and then give me two hours of your day and I promise that if you really hate it, I will bring you straight home."

"That's what Kendra and Millie said to me last night and look how that ended up."

"I quite like how it ended up," he said.

The waitress returned with their food and Georgie continued to stare at him across the table while he waited for her reply. He was nervous that she would turn him down, something he hadn't felt in a while.

She huffed out a resigned sigh and picked up her knife and fork, cutting into her bacon with gusto. "Okay, fine," she said, stuffing the bacon in her mouth, "I'll go with you, but I refuse to get changed so this will have to do."

He grinned as he attended to his own breakfast. "I would never ask you to change," he said and he knew it to the tips of his toes to be the truth. Seeing her all glammed up last night had been a surprise and he'd liked the view, but he preferred Georgie in her natural state. She was perfect just as she was.

GEORGIE COULDN'T BELIEVE that she had agreed to go with Connor on this mystery adventure. Just the thought of the outdoors gave her hives and it wasn't because she was some prima donna. She was just so clumsy and bad things could happen to clumsy people in the outdoors. And there were bears. Okay, there weren't any bears in Australia, but there were other things that were dangerous. Wasn't there a meme somewhere about everything in Australia trying to kill you? It wasn't far from the truth as far as she was concerned.

Connor reached over the console of his truck and took her hand in his, squeezing it gently.

"You look terrified," he said.

"You do remember who I am don't you?" Georgie said, looking at him and silently loving the feel of his hand in hers, "I'm the girl who trips over her own feet."

"I promise that what we're going to do isn't dangerous."

"It doesn't matter," she said shaking her head, "I'm a klutz and what about wild animals? Crocodiles and snakes and spiders and such. I'm pretty sure even wombats are vicious."

"Okay, for one, there are no crocodiles in the Northern Tablelands, you're thinking of Northern Queensland. Two, snakes are just as scared of us as we are of them. If you leave them alone, they'll leave you alone and thirdly, I really don't think spiders are going to be an issue."

"What about the wombats?"

"Wombats are slow, you could outrun one."

"Ha ha, very funny. I don't run."

"Not even a little bit?"

"If you see me running then you better run too because something is chasing me."

He laughed and the joyous sound filled the cab of the truck and made her skin prickle in a delicious way.

"You should put that on a t-shirt," he said.

"I think I already have it on a shirt," she replied and he laughed again.

"So where are we going?" she asked when the cab was quiet again.

"It's a surprise," he replied, squeezing her hand again.

She liked that he was holding her hand and she was in no hurry to break the contact. Instead she leaned back in the comfortable leather seat and watched the scenery go by. It really was a beautiful part of the country. Some people thought the Australian bush was harsh, but there was a stark beauty about it. This part of the world was a dichotomy of grassy grazing paddocks and rocky scrub. Large boulders covered in moss and lichen seemed to sprout out of nowhere and the tall gum trees stood like majestic sentries, their white trunks and grey/green leaves striking against the cyan blue of the sky.

After a while, Connor turned off the main road onto a bumpy dirt track. They trundled along, slower now, as he navigated the rough road that was little more than a goat track until finally pulling up under a tree in a cleared spot that had some semblance to a parking lot.

"Come on," he said, getting out of the truck and heading to the back of the tray.

Georgie climbed down from her side and shut the door firmly before joining him at the back of the truck. He plonked a wide-brimmed hat on her head. It was an Akubra and it was pink, which she appreciated. Then he handed her a bottle of water and held up a bottle of sunscreen. At her nod, he smeared some of the pungent smelling stuff over her nose before doing his own face and shoulders. He was wearing a tank top and those very muscled shoulders were on display. She looked away before she could make a fool of herself.

The tail gate slammed shut and he took her hand, pulling her toward a break in the trees.

"Come on," he said, "It's time for your first adventure into the great outdoors."

6

Georgie was exhausted. She couldn't remember ever walking so far or for so long. She was sweaty, her feet hurt and she was pretty sure she was sunburnt, but despite all that, she was having fun. Connor had kept her entertained with his silly antics and stupid dad jokes and she hadn't once thought about bugs or snakes or wombats. Who knew a walk in the bush could be so fun?

"Here we are," Connor said, coming to a stop.

Georgie stepped up beside him and took a deep breath taking in the incredible view.

"Wow," she breathed.

The vista spread out below them, a mix of rocky outcroppings and untamed scrub. There wasn't a building or a road in sight and the stillness of the midday bush was calming. Hardly a leaf stirred as nocturnal animals slumbered and the sun-loving ones took an afternoon siesta in the heat of the day. Georgie sat on a rock and soaked in the view, never having ever seen anything so beautiful or so perfect.

"Thank you," she said, turning to Connor and giving him a small smile.

"For what?" he asked, sitting beside her.

"For making me come, for bringing me here to see this."

He looked out at the view and she studied his profile. He really was the most handsome man she had ever seen in real life. How was it that she got to be here with him? She was not exactly the type of girl that stuff like this happened to. Georgie was a nobody, one of those people that blended into the background. Her own parents barely remembered that she was alive, so how was it possible that Connor Faulkes had come into her life?

"Come on," he said, getting to his feet and pulling her up.

"Can't we stay here a little bit longer?"

"I want to show you something."

Georgie bent at the waist to touch her toes and stretch out her legs before reaching up and stretching her arms above her head.

"Okay," she said, following him back down the trail.

The walked in silence for a bit, back the way they came and then Connor took a detour down a narrow track that she hadn't even noticed the first time.

"Where are we going?" she asked, not exactly nervous, but not real confident either.

"It's a surprise," he said, turning to look at her over his shoulder and giving her a wink.

"I don't like surprises," she said.

"Who doesn't like surprises?" he asked, coming to a stop and turning to face her.

"Me," she said with a shrug. "Surprises, in my experience, are never good things."

"Never had a surprise party?"

She snorted and shook her head, "People would actually have to care about me to organise a surprise party."

"Your parents never threw you a party or surprised you with a gift or took you on a trip?"

"I went to an all-girls boarding school and spent my holidays at camps and for my birthday I would get money or gift vouchers which were to be spent on educational pursuits."

He gaped at her. "You're not serious."

"I'm completely serious," she said.

"Okay, well, that has to change. I'm taking you somewhere that is going to show you that all surprises don't have to be bad."

He took her hand and pulled her down the trail and she let him, surprised by her confession to him about her parents. Georgie never talked about them, mainly because it made her sad. They didn't approve of her 'little bookshop hobby' as they called it and were waiting for her to stop 'procrastinating' and get a 'proper' job.

They were both scientists, her mother working in a lab that was trying to cure Cystic Fibrosis and her father a sought after lecturer who regularly published papers on genetic engineering and cloning. Georgie had always felt that she was just another one of their experiments. An experiment that they weren't too happy with the outcome.

"And here we are," Connor said, breaking through her morose thoughts.

In front of them was a small lake, the water reflecting the blue sky and shimmering in the sunlight. It looked so inviting and Georgie wished she had her bathing suit.

"What is this place?"

"It's a billabong."

"No," she said looking at Connor in surprise, "Really?"

"Really."

"I thought they were only myths. Wait. Does that mean there might be a bunyip nearby?"

He laughed, the rich sound echoing around them and making Georgie smile, lifting the melancholia that had descended on her at the thought of her parents.

"No bunyips, I don't think, but this really is a billabong."

Georgie sat down and began removing her shoes.

"What are you doing?" Connor asked.

"It's hot, I'm hot and my feet hurt and the water looks good so I thought I would dangle my feet in for a bit."

He sat down beside her and started doing the same. When her feet were bare, she walked down to the edge where a rock ledge leaned over the water, and sat down, plunging her feet into the cool water. She closed her eyes and luxuriated in the blissful feeling. She felt Connor sit beside her and it felt nice to have someone to share this with. She had been a loaner for so long, never really fitting in anywhere or with anyone. It felt good to have a small breath of time where she felt normal, and she had Connor to thank for that.

"So, do you still hate surprises?"

She opened her eyes and looked at him with a smile, "I don't love them, but this whole day has gone a long way to proving to me that they're not all bad."

"Good," he said and then pushed her in.

The cool water closed over her and the shock of him pushing her in had her spluttering as she surfaced. Before he could stop laughing, she grabbed a hold of his leg and pulled, causing him to over balance and fall into the water too. Then it was her turn to laugh and any remaining vestiges of melancholy were washed away.

CONNOR COULDN'T BELIEVE she'd actually pulled him in. It was so unlike her, but he couldn't say he didn't like it. He had planned on jumping in after her anyway, but wanted to see how she would react first. If he had done that to any of the other women he'd dated in the past, he would've been given the cold shoulder and an icy glare because he had dared disturb their perfectly coiffed hairstyle and made their artfully applied makeup run. But Georgie didn't give a second thought to either of those things.

He watched her as she laughed at him and something warmed

his insides. The unfettered joy on her face was something to behold and he wanted to keep it there. Things had gotten a little serious on the trail when she was talking about her childhood. It was a childhood he couldn't even imagine and he hadn't liked seeing her sad. Pushing her in the water had been a spur of the moment thing, but now he was glad he did it, especially since it put that smile on her face.

He swam towards her and she splashed him, drenching him with a sheet of water.

"That was mean Connor," she said as she kicked away from him.

"But fun, right?"

"I thought you were trying to show me good surprises."

He edged closer to her. "Come on, that was a good surprise."

She splashed at him again, but this time he grabbed hold of her hands and pulled her towards him, trapping her in his arms. Their bodies bumped under the water and Georgie looked up at him with her big blue eyes, her glasses wet but miraculously still in place, and her eyelashes starred with water drops.

His gaze dropped to her mouth, the lush, pink lips devoid of makeup, wet from the water of the billabong and unerringly kissable. She bit the corner of her lip and he raised his eyes to hers, the sparkle of laughter gone but something even more appealing in its place. The moment spun out between them as he held her, the sounds of the bush around them and the quiet lapping of the water as the ripples they created reached the edge of the billabong. He wanted to kiss her, but he didn't want to rush it. This setting, this moment was too precious to ruin by moving too fast.

Slowly he lowered his head towards her, his eyes never leaving hers until her lashes fluttered shut. He was mere breaths away from his lips touching hers when he felt her stiffen and it gave him pause. Before he could taste her lips, she was pushing away from him, swimming across the billabong to the rock where they had been sitting earlier. He stayed where he was, watching as she pulled herself out of the water and up onto the rock, wringing out her wet hair and clothes.

To say he was stunned was an understatement. He was flummoxed and confused. He'd been sure she had felt the moment just as he did and that she'd wanted the kiss as much as him. Now he was left with a feeling of unfinished business, an opportunity missed, and he didn't know if she would ever let him get that close again.

He made his way back across the water to the rock where she was now lying, soaking in the warmth of the sun in what he suspected was an attempt to dry herself and her clothes. He pulled himself up beside her and she flinched, but didn't move away. He knew that he would have to take these next steps carefully or she was liable to run away like a frightened rabbit. He could see the tension in her body as she pretended to be calm. Instead of asking her why, she stopped him from kissing her (which was what he really wanted to do), he pulled off his wet shirt and wrung it out over her supine body, drenching her again.

She sat up in surprise and slapped at him while he laughed, faking humour and trying to put her at ease once more.

"Thanks for that," she said as she tried to once again wring out her wet clothes.

"Anytime," he said with a grin.

He knew the moment she realised he was bare chested and had to stifle a laugh at her response. Her eyes widened and she swallowed, her gaze drawn to the flexed muscles of his pecs and abs. Connor worked hard on his body, it was in his contracts to be in the best physical shape possible and so he knew he looked good. And, to be honest, he liked it when women appreciated his efforts. Seeing Georgie's cheeks flush as she stared at him, though, that was something else. He wanted to preen for her, flex and pose like some oiled-up body builder in order to show off for her. He didn't, although the desire to was strong.

"We should probably get going," she said, her voice a bit deeper, a bit breathier.

"Sure," he said, for the first time seeing how her wet clothes moulded to her body and feeling his mouth go dry.

Georgie was petite, but still curvy, unlike the women he'd dated in the past. He couldn't deny he liked the female form, whatever shape it took, but it was a refreshing change to see a woman who wasn't all bones and lean muscles. The women he normally dated were models or actresses or socialites hoping to be actresses and they all had punishing workout schedules, just as he did, in their attempt to chase their dreams. He figured Georgie had never seen the inside of a gym or ran for miles on a treadmill and he liked the effect.

She stood to her feet and walked over to where they had left their shoes, water bottles, and mobile phones. She slipped her shoes on and then stood waiting for him. Reluctantly, not ready for their day to end, he got to his feet and followed suit.

He liked everything about her, from her long tangled hair to her cute little feet with blue nail polish on the toes and that was dangerous. Connor knew that getting involved with her was the wrong thing to do. He was only here for a couple more weeks and then after that he would be shooting on location for months and didn't know when he would be back in Australia, let alone Oxley Crossing. Starting something with her would be a bad idea and yet he was helpless to stop the feelings swirling around inside him. He wanted to spend time with her, to know what made her smile and what made her sad. He wanted to know more about how she grew up and what her parents were like and what her hopes and dreams were. He wanted to kiss her, to know what her lips tasted like as he sipped from them, learning their shape and their softness and feeling her body sigh against his. He wanted all of that and more than he wanted his next breath.

. . .

THEY FOLLOWED THE TRAIL BACK, Connor letting Georgie lead. It wasn't his greatest idea, but she appreciated the gesture. They didn't get lost, well, not exactly anyway, and eventually they came out to the car park, though via a different trail.

The car park that had been empty when they began their adventure now had a rather large motorhome filling up two parking spaces and as they broke through the trees and into the open, the door opened and a middle-aged couple descended the steps.

"Oh my goodness," the woman said, rushing over to them. Georgie was immediately on edge and froze as the woman bee-lined for them. "You're Connor Faulkes."

Georgie relaxed slightly as the woman pushed past her, not even acknowledging her existence. She was a little offended for Connor's sake. As for Georgie, she was used to being ignored.

"Marilyn," the man called to her, "Leave these nice folks alone."

Marilyn waved a distracted hand at, who Georgie assumed was, her husband and stared up at Connor like he was an ice cream cone melting in the sun and she desperately wanted to lick him.

"You are Connor Faulkes aren't you?"

"Yes, ma'am," Connor responded with a grin.

"I knew it! Can I have a photo with you?"

Connor shot Georgie an apologetic glance as the woman snuggled up beside him and extended her phone on a selfie-stick so that she could take the photo.

"I apologise for my wife," the man said coming to stand beside Georgie, "I think she's been going a bit stir crazy since we started our trip. We've never really spent this much time together without other people in the mix."

"How long have you been on the road?"

"A little over a month now. It was always our dream to retire and join the ranks of the grey nomads, but I'm not so sure it's going to work out."

The grey nomads was what the country affectionately called retired couples who sold everything up and spent six months or so of the year travelling around Australia in motor homes and caravans. It sounded idyllic to Georgie, but then she was a bit of a loner and would find the solitude blissful.

"Harry stop gas-bagging and get over here and take a photo of me and Connor Faulkes!"

Harry sighed indulgently and went to do his wife's bidding. Georgie didn't envy him spending twenty-four hours a day cooped up in a motorhome with Marilyn, though. She seemed like a handful.

The woman continued to monopolise Connor, always calling him 'Connor Faulkes' like he couldn't simply be just Connor. Connor, for the most part, smiled politely and chatted to the couple asking about their travels and their family. He even tried to include her in the conversation, introducing her to Marilyn and Harry, but Marilyn continued to ignore her. Eventually, after signing his autograph numerous times on whatever she could find in her motor home, Connor managed to disentangle himself from the older woman, who had a death grip on his arm, and he came over to Georgie, slung his arm around her shoulder and whispered in her ear.

"Quick. Let's make a break for it."

They walked determinedly to the car, but didn't run in case it spooked Marilyn and she came running after them. They got in the car and Connor backed out of the parking space and drove sedately away, waving to Marilyn over his shoulder. They didn't speak until they hit the main road and then Georgie laughed.

"Oh my God! Does that happen often?"

He sighed ruefully, "At home it does, but I'm usually safe when I come here. The locals know me and kind of protect me from the prying eyes of the media and I don't usually run into many tourists."

"You were really sweet to her," Georgie said with a soft smile, a warm feeling of affection filling her. Connor looked at the road and Georgie swore his cheeks turned a little pink under his tan. Was the great Connor Faulkes blushing?

"Do people always call you by your full name?"

He groaned. "Fans do. My name has become like a brand name, but I suppose it's the same with most actors. Like Tom Cruise, Chris Pine, George Clooney. If I just said Tom, Chris and George then you wouldn't know who I was talking about."

"But still... you are a person behind your name and it's kind of weird to call you 'Connor Faulkes' like you can't be Connor without the identifier of your last name."

He shrugged. "People want to meet the movie star, not the man."

"I suppose," she mused, "I think I like the man better."

He shot her a look and his mouth quirked in a grin. "Are you admitting you like me?"

"Oh God," she said dropping her head and blushing furiously.

He laughed, the sound filling the cab and rippling over her skin. "Georgie likes me," he cooed.

"Now you're pushing it," she said, but there was no heat in her voice.

"Na ah, you can't take it back," he said, his wide smile splitting his face and his eyes sparkling. Then he sobered just a little. The smile was still on his face, but not as wide, and his eyes darkened as he shot her a quick glance before turning back to the road. "I like you too, Georgie," he said, reaching across the console and taking her hand in his.

All the girlie bits inside Georgie broke out into cheering and applause making her heart race and her head spin. Connor Faulkes liked her, she thought and then gave herself a mental slap. Connor, the man, liked her and that was even better.

❧ 7 ❧

Georgie sat in Book Club trying really hard not to stare at Connor. Since their little adventure to the billabong, he had been a regular visitor at Bookish, picking up new books for Dawn, staying to have coffee and a chat with her while devouring her freshly baked muffins. She knew that her regular customers had noticed. They hadn't said anything to her directly, but she saw the knowing looks and the smiles. Even now as she sat in Book Club with an argument going on about Jordan Wicks' motivations for his actions, the attraction between them felt palpable and Dawn had a very 'cat that ate the canary' look on her face.

As much as she had come to like Connor since getting to know the man behind the Prince Charming persona, she knew that it couldn't turn into anything long lasting. They were from two different worlds and they were not worlds that could be easily blended. Not that she thought Connor had forever on his mind. They got along well and were friends; however, she was a bit of a distraction for him while he was here and that was the extent of their relationship.

She steadfastly refused to think about the near kiss when they were in the billabong except she was kidding herself, because she couldn't get it out of her mind. Would he have really kissed her if she hadn't gotten spooked? She didn't have any experience with real-life relationships between men and women and was ashamed to admit that at the tender age of twenty-four, she had never been kissed. She was a romance book trope. The only thing she knew about kissing was what she read about, and she had read a lot. All the signs had been there; the way he looked at her, how his eyes had dropped to her lips, the way his arms had tightened around her. It was all textbook, the romance story prelude to a kiss. And it had freaked her out.

She bit her lip as she remembered the moment that had seemed to stretch out and slow down around them and her eyes met Connor's across the Book Club circle. The intensity in his gaze made her wonder if he was thinking about that moment too. Was he remembering how well they seemed to fit together? Was he thinking about how it felt like they were in a dream world where only the two of them existed?

The sudden silence in the room had her tuning back in to the present. All eyes were on her and she swallowed, feeling like an idiot for letting herself daydream while in a room full of the worst of the town's gossips.

"Ah, where were we?"

Kendra hid her smile behind her hand and Connor grinned at her, his eyes sparkling with humour.

"We were asking about next week," Dawn provided helpfully.

"Right," Georgie said feeling flustered and out of sorts. "I think it's time we moved on to book two, what do you say?"

A round of nods and murmured agreements and then everyone was packing up and making their goodbyes. She sat there, mortified to have been caught, but unable to make her getaway. She didn't want to leave yet and didn't have to go back to the shop that afternoon. Millie had taken on Wednesdays so she could do Book Club and it left her afternoon blissfully free.

Usually she would be heading directly to her apartment for a long, leisurely afternoon with a good book or a sappy movie. Today, she wanted to stay here.

"Georgie," Dawn said after everyone was gone, "why don't you stay for lunch?"

"Oh, I couldn't. I don't want to be a bother. We already take up so much of your time with Book Club."

"Nonsense," Dawn said, "I love having Book Club here. You're the one who has gone out of her way to accommodate an old lady. Let me thank you by giving you lunch."

Georgie shot a look to Connor who had just walked back in the room, flicking his keys around his finger.

"All right Gran?" he asked.

Dawn smiled at her grandson, "I'm good," she said, "I was just asking Georgie to stay for lunch. Are you going out?"

He looked down at the keys in his hand and then at Georgie and she knew. He was leaving.

"I have to go in to Armidale for a meeting," he said, his eyes leaving Georgie's and making contact with Dawn's. "Will you be all right on your own for a couple of hours?"

"Can't you stay for lunch, dear?"

He looked at his watch, but didn't look back at Georgie. "I really need to go."

"You have to eat," Dawn said.

"I'll grab something on the way," Connor said and then turned to walk out of the room, "I'll see you tonight."

Connor walked out and left Georgie staring after him in confusion. He hadn't even said good bye to her and seemed like he couldn't get out of the house fast enough. Had she done something to upset him? Or had he just come to realise that they really had nothing in common?

"Help me up, dear," Dawn said, struggling to get out of her recliner, "And let's have some lunch."

. . .

CONNOR POUNDED on his steering wheel in frustration. He had handled that badly, but he didn't know what he could have done differently. He did have a meeting in Armidale, although it wasn't until later He just needed to get out of Georgie's orbit before he did something that they'd both regret.

He couldn't deny the attraction he felt towards her. It was an attraction that was growing day by day the more he spent time with her. He'd overheard Gran invite her to lunch and he knew that if he didn't get out of the house, he was going to take things with her to the next logical step and if he did that then they were both going to get hurt. He was leaving in a couple of weeks and starting something with her would end badly. If the paparazzi ever got wind of her, her life would be ruined and he didn't want that for her. She guarded her privacy and he respected that. He knew what he was getting into when he pursued this career, but Georgie didn't ask for any of it and she shouldn't be punished for his fame.

That didn't make walking away any easier, though. He'd barely been able to keep his eyes off her during Book Club and then when she'd started to lose attention on the discussion, he knew what she'd been thinking about. It had been written all over her face. She was thinking about what had nearly happened in the billabong and that made him think about it and remember how right she felt in his arms. He had wanted to kiss her in that moment and still wanted to kiss her. But if he did, if he let things go that far, he would be making a promise he couldn't keep. There was no future for the two of them, despite what he might hope for. They were on parallel tracks, running side by side but never destined to cross. It was something he needed to keep reminding himself.

"SO, YOU AND CONNOR, HUH?"

Georgie blushed. "We're just friends."

Dawn laughed, "It looked a lot more than that."

"No, really," Georgie insisted, "We are just friends. There's nothing going on between us. Besides, he's Connor Faulkes and I'm, well, I'm just me."

Dawn reached across the table and squeezed Georgie's hand.

"I've never seen him look at anyone the way he was looking at you today."

"That's sweet to say," Georgie said, "But it's impossible. We are so different and come from such different lives. He has his movies and his fame and I have Bookish."

"Those are not insurmountable obstacles," Dawn said.

Georgie shrugged. "What would I do in his world? He dates celebrities and models. Women who are tall and gorgeous and know how to wear designer clothes. I'm a bookshop owner with a penchant for quirky shirts and Converse shoes."

"And he's just a man who thinks you're pretty and likes being around you. I know where he goes during the day, I know how much time the two of you have been spending together. Why not just relax and let whatever is going to happen, happen?"

Georgie patted Dawn's hand. "It's a lovely dream," she said, "But that's all it is, a fairytale. Connor is Prince Charming and I'm just a fun distraction to keep him occupied while he is in town."

"You're selling yourself short," Dawn said with a shake of her head, "You're selling him short. Besides, what's the harm in having fun for the short time that he is here? Not every relationship has to be forever. If you like him and he likes you, what's to stop you from taking it a day at a time? If nothing else, you'll be making memories that will last you a lifetime."

Maybe Dawn was right. Georgie had never even had a boyfriend, so why was she thinking in terms of forevermore? Admittedly having Connor Faulkes as her first boyfriend was a steep learning curve, but hey, why not? She could look at it as an experiment, and wouldn't her parents be proud? She was bound to learn something and the experience would be good for her. She may even get her first kiss out of the deal and when Connor left, they could even stay friends. She could be his pen pal, and they could keep in touch via email and Skype, wherever he was in the world.

It sounded like a good plan, so why did she feel so rotten?

❧ 8 ❧

Sleep eluded Connor. He couldn't stop thinking about the flash of hurt that had crossed Georgie's face when he'd skipped out on lunch after Book Club. Telling himself that nothing could happen between them and that he needed to keep his distance did nothing to stop the desire he had to see her. Quite simply, he enjoyed her company. His lame attempt to put distance between them had hurt her and was hurting him too.

Disgusted with himself and finally giving up on sleep, he dragged himself out of bed and pulled on a pair of sweat pants before heading to the kitchen. His meeting in Armidale had gone well and there was lots for him to read over before he committed to anything, so now was a good a time as any to start.

Connor was surprised to see his Gran awake. It was barely dawn and there she sat at the kitchen table, her crutches propped up beside her and a cup of tea in front of her. She looked up and smiled at him as he walked in.

"Kettle's just boiled," she said.

"Thanks," he replied walking into the spacious kitchen and making himself an instant coffee.

He joined his grandmother at the table taking note of the book she was reading.

"What number is that?"

"Three," she replied without looking up.

"Do you think there's enough in the series to make the franchise viable?"

She looked up at him then, her face thoughtful. "Each book deals with a different couple, so I think so. Your character doesn't have many scenes after the first book, just a few here and there."

Connor nodded, "Yeah, I knew that. Which actually kind of suits me fine."

"Oh?" Gran raised her eyebrows at him in interest, "Care to share?"

He smiled and shook his head, "It's early days yet. I'll tell you more when I know more."

"Does it have anything to do with your appointment in Armidale?"

"Maybe," he said, getting up to make himself another cup of coffee.

"Does that mean you might be around a bit more?"

"You're like a dog with a bone, aren't you?" he asked as he came back to the table and sat down.

"I miss you," she said, "And..."

"And?"

"I like having you around and I'm not the only one."

"Gran," he said, exasperation in his voice.

"I like seeing the two of you together," she said, "She's good for you and you seem to be good for her too."

He looked down at the mug in his hands, unsure what to say.

"I'm not saying you have to marry the girl," Gran said, "Just..."

He looked up at her when she paused. Her eyes were soft and compassionate and he felt a rush of affection for her.

"Just don't give up on the possibilities. Why not take it a day at a time, while you're here. Get to know her."

He sighed. He wanted that, he did, but he was worried. "I don't want her to get attached to me and then when I leave, she gets hurt."

"But she knows you're leaving, so shouldn't she at least be given the choice? You pulling away from her because you think it's the right thing to do doesn't give her any say in the matter."

"I just thought I'd save us both a bit of heartache."

Gran smiled softly at him. "And has it?"

He shook his head, both in acknowledgement of her question and his awe at her perception.

"The press would eat her alive."

"Why do they need to find out?"

"They always find out."

Gran shrugged, "It seems to me you're looking for problems before they even become problems. If the press—"

"When, Gran. It's *when* the press find out."

"Okay fine. *When* the press find out, we'll deal with it then. Until that time, why not just relax and enjoy yourself. Take a pretty girl out on a date. Laugh, dance, share a meal and some good conversation. You might even get the chance to kiss her goodnight."

Connor smiled to himself. What was the harm in it? They had already gone out on their bushwalking adventure and nothing dreadful had happened. In fact it had been kind of wonderful and he very nearly got to kiss her. He knew he couldn't rush things with her, but a goodnight kiss after a date would be expected, wouldn't it? Especially if the date went as well as their bushwalking had gone.

"Fine," he said, smiling at Gran, "I'll ask her out on a date. Where do you suggest I take her?"

His Gran smiled victoriously and he had the feeling he'd just been had, but the joy that had suffused him when he had decided to ask Georgie out chased away any misgivings he might have had. So what if Gran had subtly manipulated him into asking Georgie out? It wasn't a hardship by any stretch of the imagination. He *wanted* to take her out on a date.

Connor stood outside Bookish and watched Georgie as she helped old Mrs. Thompson. It was a little bit stalkerish, but he didn't often get the chance to watch her in her natural environment. He knew as soon as he walked through the door, Georgie would change. It wasn't arrogance that led him to that conclusion, but knowledge. There was something between them, something undeniable. Whenever they were in each other's air space, the chemistry between them arced, making them both behave differently. Unfortunately it made Georgie self-conscious and clumsy. For him, though, it was another story. Whenever he was around her, he felt more alive. His skin became super sensitive, his hearing sharpened and his eyes were drawn to her like magnets.

The shop door opened and Millie walked out, giving him a knowing glance.

"Connor," she said, "What are you doing here?"

"I've come to see Georgie," he answered truthfully.

Millie crossed her arms and stared him down. "I hope you're here to apologise."

"She told you?"

"Of course not, but I'm her friend and I know when she's upset about something. The only thing she could be upset about is you. What did you do?"

"I was an idiot," he confessed.

"Lead with that," she said, "I hope you have a plan to make it up to her."

"I do," he said.

"Good."

They both turned to see Georgie say good bye to Mrs. Thompson and head over to the coffee machine to serve another customer. He liked watching her when she was at ease, the way she confidently moved about her space, a smile on her face as she spoke to her patrons.

"Well, go on," Millie said, "I'll cover for her while you apologise."

He took a deep breath and stepped into the shop. She knew exactly when he crossed the threshold, he could see her shoulders tense and her smile become more forced. He hated that he'd done that, that the ease they had found with one another had been disturbed because of his stupidity. Millie pushed him from behind, reminding him that he hadn't come to stand in the door way. He moved into the shop and over towards the counter where she was handing over the coffee she had just made. He waited for her to farewell the customer before he stepped up to her. She shot him a quick glance and then turned to walk away, but he shot out his hand to take hold of hers so she couldn't leave.

"Can we talk?"

"I'm working, Connor."

He took a quick look around the shop. There were a few people in the store, but no one looked like they were in desperate need of assistance.

"I know, but what I have to say is important."

She sighed and cast her gaze anywhere but at him.

"Please?" He wasn't above begging.

"Fine," she said, "But I can't be away from the desk for too long."

He grinned and let her lead the way through the stacks to the small office she had in the back. He'd never been in the tiny room before and there was barely enough room for the both of them and the desk which she put between them by sitting down behind it.

She looked up at him expectantly, but didn't say anything. He cleared his throat.

"I was an idiot," he said, deciding that Millie was right. "I'm sorry for not staying for lunch the other day. I really did have an appointment in Armidale, but it's no excuse for my being rude." He sat down in the chair opposite her and beseeched her with his eyes. "We had something good between us and, well, I ruined it and I'm sorry."

"Okay," she said, drawing out the word.

"You and I both know that I'm only here for another couple of weeks and I didn't want to... I don't know how to say it without sounding like a douche."

A small smile played around her lips. "Just say it."

"I love spending time with you, Georgie, more than I have with anyone in a long time. I got scared. I was worried that if we spent more time together that you would end up getting hurt so I thought—"

"You thought you would spare me the hurt then by hurting me now."

He dropped his head and mumbled, "Yeah," ashamed of his cowardice. He took a breath and looked up at her, "But I was wrong," he said, "I was wrong to do that without talking to you first, without giving you a chance to tell me what you want. And..."

"And?"

"And, I like you and I missed you and I want to spend time with you while I can. Have dinner with me tonight."

"Is that a question or a command?"

"Wow," he said with a shake of his head, "I haven't yet met tough Georgie. I like her."

Georgie rewarded him with a bright smile that took his breath away. She was absolutely stunning when she smiled that way, it lit up her whole face and made her eyes sparkle.

"Please, Georgie, would you go out to dinner with me tonight?"

"I'd love to," she said and he could breathe again.

"I'll pick you up at six," he said, "Does that give you enough time after the shop closes?"

Georgie shrugged, "Sure," she said and then bit her lip, "Um, what should I wear? I mean, are we going to restaurant or on one of your adventure thingies?"

He smiled at her. "This is a real date," he said, "in a real restaurant with waiters and everything."

Her eyes widened in what looked a lot like trepidation, but she nodded.

"Ah, okay then, sure six is fine."

"I'll see you then," he said, getting up and walking out of the office, waving to Millie as he headed out of the store, a mile wide smile on his face.

❦ 9 ❦

"For God's sake, sit still!" Kendra admonished, but Georgie was so nervous she didn't think she could sit still.

After Connor had left, she'd had a panicked conversation with Millie who had then called Kendra. They were in her apartment, trying to get her ready for her date with Prince Charming. Who was she to be going on a date with a movie star? And what if she spilt something on her dress or knocked over the wine or did any number of stupid things that she was inclined to do? This wasn't just Connor from Book Club, this was Connor Faulkes, movie star and one of Australia's most eligible bachelors. What the heck was she, Georgie Danners, book shop owner, doing going out with him?

"Calm down," Millie said, walking into the room with a handful of wardrobe choices.

The three of them were similar sizes, although they both had more in the bra department than Georgie. Millie and Kendra had both brought a few outfits for her to try on since none of Georgie's clothes would be acceptable. She didn't think that her usual jeans and quirky t-shirt would cut it at a restaurant.

"What if I use the wrong fork?" Georgie said, suddenly reminded of the scene in Pretty Woman.

"I don't think he'll care one way or another what fork you use," Kendra said.

"But I bet he knows all about that sort of stuff. We've only seen 'good ole boy' Connor, we haven't really seen The Connor Faulkes."

"I wouldn't think there was much difference," Millie said, "He doesn't strike me as the type to pretend to be someone he's not."

"He's an actor," Georgie reminded them, "All he does is pretend he's someone he's not."

"That's his job, what he does when he's working, it's not who he is." Kendra's calm steadiness helped to soothe Georgie's jittery nerves. "You know him," she went on, "You've spent time with him, gotten to know the real Connor behind all the hype. Relax and just enjoy it, enjoy being out on a date with a gorgeous man."

Georgie stared at herself in the mirror.

"My first date," she whispered, "And it's with Connor Faulkes."

"No," Kendra said, laying a hand on her shoulder and catching her eyes in the reflection of the mirror. "Your first date with Connor, your friend."

"She's right," Millie said, coming to stand beside them, "You have to stop obsessing over him being an actor. Not once has he behaved like some toffee-nosed, entitled douchebag. You're the one who keeps bringing up his status and it's doing your head in. So stop it. You're going out on a date, your first date, with a guy who you've already spent hours with. Just relax and enjoy it."

Georgie looked at her two friends and took a deep breath. She knew they were right, but she was so nervous. It was her first date, which would give her nerves enough, but that it was with a guy that she really liked, despite him being famous, that only ratcheted up the nerves even more without adding the extra pressure of him being a movie star and gorgeous and her dream guy. It wasn't just that he was a star, it was that she had fantasised about him for so long that she had put him on a pedestal. Even getting to know him over the last few weeks hadn't diminished the awe she felt for him. If anything, her awe had grown. He was the perfect man - good looking, fit, strong, kind, sweet, nice, funny, confident - she could list his attributes for hours.

"He's just a guy," Millie said, breaking into her thoughts.

"That doesn't help," Georgie said, "I'm hopeless around all guys, twice as much around Connor."

"Maybe you were at first," Kendra said, "But I haven't seen a hint of clumsiness or awkwardness lately when he's around. You even got into a heated discussion with him at Book Club."

Georgie was surprised to realise that what Kendra was saying was right. The first few times she'd been a complete klutz, but lately she'd actually felt normal around him and hadn't even given a second thought to her awkwardness or clumsiness.

"See, it worked!" Millie crowed.

"What worked?"

"Immersion therapy."

"I thought it was exposure therapy," Georgie said dryly.

Millie waved the comment away. "Same horse, different jockey. But the fact remains, I was right. It worked."

"So I'm cured, doctor?"

"Don't be a smarty pants," Millie said, undeterred. "In this instance, you are. Being around Connor all the time has made you forget to be nervous. You're used to him and as such, no more clumsiness."

"Hmm, maybe," Georgie conceded, "But we're entering a whole new environment here. I've never been on a date with him."

"Why all the pressure on the word 'date'?" Kendra asked, "it's just the two of you having dinner, what's the big deal?"

"You guys wouldn't understand," Georgie said, nerves fading and melancholy settling in. "You've both been on lots of dates, had boyfriends and all that stuff. This is all new to me and it makes me nervous and anxious and I feel completely out of my depth."

Kendra put her arm around Georgie and gave her a squeeze. "But it's just Connor. Getting dressed up and going to a restaurant doesn't change the fact that this is Connor, your friend, the guy you've been hanging out with for weeks now. You are psyching yourself out for absolutely no reason. Now come and try on this dress, I think it will be perfect on you."

Georgie tried to let her friends' confidence rub off on her and she smiled and nodded and did all the things to make them think that she had put aside her anxiety. The fact was, as the time drew closer, she felt like her heart was going to beat out of her chest. That's who she was; she put a lot of pressure on herself and she didn't know how to change that. She just hoped that she wouldn't make a fool of herself tonight.

THERE WAS a knock on the door and Georgie felt like throwing up. He was here, this was really happening. Part of her had wondered whether he would call and cancel or even just stand her up, but no, Connor was here and she was going on a date.

Kendra and Millie had left only a few minutes ago after having primped and preened her to within an inch of her life. She wore a slinky black dress that wasn't too short, but had a side split that showed a decent amount of leg. It was backless, which in this heat wasn't a bad choice and she didn't have to worry about a bra, not with her little pimples. On her feet were scrappy silver heels that she actually really liked, but made her feel a little gangly and unsure on her legs. They had left her hair down, but instead of straightening it, Kendra had curled it into soft waves. There was no Vamp Red lipstick this time, just a pale blush colour and for the first time in ages, she was wearing contacts.

There was another hesitant knock on the door and she rolled her eyes at herself for being frozen in place. With a calming breath, she crossed the room and opened the door. Connor stood there in a dark suit with a crisp white shirt underneath that was open at the collar. He'd shaved the unruly scruff from his face, but not entirely, leaving a manicured short growth of dark blonde whiskers. He smiled when he saw her, his eyes lighting up and her nerves disappeared like smoke.

"You look beautiful," he said, his voice husky.

"So do you," she replied, her own voice breathy.

He held out his arm to her, "Shall we?"

Georgie took his arm and let him guide her down the stairs and out into the street where a sleek BMW sat waiting for them.

"Where's your truck?" She asked.

"I figured you wouldn't want to be climbing up into it with a dress and heels on," he said with a shy shrug, "So I borrowed Gran's car."

"Thank you," she said, feeling touched by his thoughtfulness.

He opened the car door for her and she slid into the soft leather seat. He rounded the car and slid behind the wheel and then they were pulling away from the curb.

"Where are we going?" she asked as they passed out of town.

"I've heard some good things about Window Payne Wineries and I thought we could check it out."

"Nice," she said relaxing into the seat, "I haven't been there, but I've wanted to."

"Do you know the Payne brothers?" he asked.

She shook her head. "No. Kendra might, she grew up here."

"I was friends with them back in the day," he said, "I'm excited to see what they've done with the property. It wasn't a vineyard back then, just rolling hills and some old out buildings."

They lapsed into a comfortable silence for the rest of the journey.

SHE WAS STUNNING. Sitting opposite him in the soft candlelight he couldn't help but notice just how beautiful she was. It wasn't the clothes or the makeup or even the fact that she wasn't wearing her glasses tonight, it was just her. Everything about her. Her golden hair shone in the low light and her eyes were like the sparkling cerulean sea. Her fair skin had a rosy glow from the wine and her lips were plush and pink and he wanted to taste them. She had him bewitched and it wasn't something she'd said or done, it was just her and he knew he was lost. Just the fact that he was thinking such poetic things was testament to how much she had affected him.

"So what are your plans?" she asked, sipping from her wine glass, "I know you've got 'A Royal Engagement' coming up, but what then, after that?"

"I've got a new venture in the works," he said, wanting to share his news with her, "A local project."

Her eyebrows lifted up elegantly. "Here in Aus?"

He nodded. "I want to try my hand at directing," he said, "That's what the meeting in Armidale was all about. I met with an independent film studio who pitched me an idea. I'd have a small role in it, but what I'm really interested in is the chance to get behind the camera."

She smiled at him, a genuine delighted smile. "That sounds amazing," she said, "I don't know how you do it, I wouldn't know the first thing about making a film."

He shrugged, "I didn't either when I first started. But the more I learned the more it fascinated me. Getting the chance to work with a small independent crew will mean I'll get to learn even more."

"Surely one of the major film studios would be willing to give you a chance?"

He shook his head, "I don't want that. I know the pressure the studios put on their directors. Every movie costs an obscene amount of money and the studios need to make that money back at the box office. Plus, all of the hands on stuff would be done by several hundreds of assistants and tech support staff. I don't want that, I want to get into the thick of it, get my hands dirty, have more control. I don't want to make a movie just to make money, I want to make a movie that means something to me even if only a few people see it."

Her smile softened as she looked at him. "You're amazing," she said.

"No," he replied, "I'm just me and I can be stubborn and unreasonable and just as pigheaded as the next guy. But for the first time in a long time, I'm excited for what's coming up. Don't get me wrong, I love my job, I love acting and I'm so thankful for all the opportunities it has given me, but I'm ready for something more, something new."

She reached across the table and laid her hand on his. "I think it's wonderful and I think you're amazing. There is so much passion and energy about you that floors me sometimes. I grew up without ever experiencing anything like that and being around you inspires me."

He turned his hand over so that they were palm to palm. "Thank you," he said, touched by her words.

A waiter approached and subtly put the leather bill folder on the table. Connor glanced up and realised they were the only two left in the restaurant. Wow, where had the time gone? Being with Georgie was like being in an alternate universe where time moved differently.

He signed the check and then stood, holding his arm out to Georgie. She hooked her hand under his elbow and they walked out of the restaurant and into the balmy night.

"That was wonderful," she said as they drove down the driveway and onto the road. "The food was amazing and the wine," she smiled, "the wine was delicious."

"It was nice," he said thinking that it was the company that had made the evening so wonderful. He couldn't even remember what he ate, although it must have been good because he had such a feeling of satisfaction that only good food and wine could give.

He reached across the console and took her hand in his, liking the contact, the connection with her. The ride back to her apartment was quiet, but companionably so and far too short. He didn't want the evening to end, despite them already having spent hours together. He could quite comfortably spend many more hours with her, which gave him an idea. Instead of stopping in front of her apartment, he continued to drive through town.

"Where are we going?" Georgie asked.

"I want to show you something. Is that okay?"

He shot her a quick glance and saw her smile and nod.

It didn't take long to get to his destination and he was grateful that it was deserted. He parked the car and switched off the lights, leaving them in darkness. Looking out the windscreen the town of Oxley Crossing was laid out before them and above them was the night sky dotted with stars that looked like diamonds flung carelessly across black velvet.

"Wow," Georgie breathed, "it's beautiful."

"Come on," he said, getting out of the car and crossing to open her door.

He held her hand as they walked to the railing of the lookout. It was a clear night and they could see for miles. The twinkling lights of the small town looked like a fairy land and the sky above made them both feel like they were standing on the edge of the universe.

Unable to stop himself, Connor pulled Georgie into his arms. She looked up at him with soft, trusting eyes and he felt his heart skip a beat. Slowly, so as not to scare her away, he lowered his head, hesitating a breath from her lips to give her time to object and then he kissed her. It was a soft brush of lips that made her melt into him and he let himself get lost in the magic of it. The perfect kiss with the perfect girl on the perfect night. It was the stuff of movies, but for once in his life, it was real.

❧ 10 ☙

"Could it be that one of Australia's most eligible bachelors is off the market?"

Connor rolled his eyes at the headline as he walked passed the doorway of Gran's TV room. The entertainment news shows always made things sound so dramatic and he wondered who the poor celebrity was this time. He was lucky to have a fairly good rapport with the paps and they left him alone for the most part. He knew that as a celebrity, he owed his fans a look into his private life and he was willing to give the media shots of him in his everyday life as long as they respected his boundaries. So far it had worked and he was thankful for it.

"Connor," Gran called, "could you come in here for a minute?"

"Just a sec," he said as he poured a cup of coffee and then headed towards the sound of his grandmother's voice.

"What's up?"

She didn't say anything, just pointed to the television. A photo of him and Georgie filled the screen. It was the day they went hiking and they were laughing at something, smiling at each other, their hands touching.

"Connor Faulkes, Australia's own Prince Charming, was

spotted recently with this mystery woman. Witnesses say they were out hiking when he stopped to give a tourist an autograph and a picture—" the picture on the screen changed to the one he'd taken with Marilyn "—on her blog Ms. Luttrell said that he had been sweet to her and that he was 'such a lovely young man'. More photos have come to light of Connor and this new woman in his life—" the picture changed again to one of him and Georgie at the restaurant last night. They were gazing across the table at one another completely oblivious to everyone else around them. They looked like they were in love. "—Our sources tell us that he is in the Northern Tablelands looking after his grandmother as she recuperates from a fall. Is this mystery woman someone from his past? An old flame rekindled perhaps? If a picture is worth a thousand words then that one is saying that Connor Faulkes is in love. Sorry ladies, it looks like Prince Charming has met his Princess."

Connor had his phone in his hand before the presenter had finished speaking and it was only then that he noticed the half a dozen missed calls from his PR assistant. He hit the speed dial and waited impatiently for it to connect.

"What the heck, Tina? Why couldn't you gag this story?"

"And hello to you too," she said. "It came out of nowhere, Connor, there was nothing I could do."

"Well, you need to do something about it now. I don't want these pictures out there."

"It's too late. It's already been picked up by the US and it's gone viral on the net."

Connor swore colourfully under his breath. "Can we at least keep Georgie's name out of it?"

"I'll do my best," she said, "But you know how these things go. Someone will recognise her and give a tip to one of the tabloids. Be prepared for the invasion of press. Better yet get out of town."

"I can't just leave," he said, "And I wouldn't abandon Georgie to the sharks like that."

"So take her with you."

He shoved a hand through his hair as he thought through the logistics of that. He knew Georgie would want to run away from all this, but that would only make the paps bay for blood. They had to face this head on. If they ran, the press would only chase them, but if they rode it out, maybe it would pass quickly. There was bound to be another juicy story out there just waiting to be discovered. His love life seriously didn't deserve all this attention.

"I'll sort it from my end," he said into the phone, "But I don't want Georgie dragged into this. Do what you can to keep her name out of it for as long as possible."

He disconnected and turned to look at his Gran who had rewound and paused the news story on the photo do him and Georgie at dinner.

"That is a lovely photo," she said, "Do you think I could get a copy of it?"

"Gran," he said, exasperated.

"What? It's such a lovely shot of the two of you."

"It is," he said, "But it shouldn't be on a trashy television entertainment show, or splashed all over the internet. Georgie didn't sign up for this and she is going to hate me."

"I think Georgie knew the risks when she agreed to go out with you," Gran said, "Give her a bit more credit. You don't know how she is going to react."

"Oh, I think I do," he said under his breath. He knew Georgie hated being in the spotlight and he knew this would send her into hiding. Everything that he'd tried to accomplish with her was ruined with one photograph. There was no way Georgie would want to have anything to do with him after this and his only option now was damage control.

The phone in his hand rang and he didn't recognise the international number. He hit the ignore button, but he knew it was just the tip of the iceberg. If someone from the international press had his private cell number, then it wouldn't be long before everyone had it. He sent a quick text to Tina and then to his agent before turning off his phone. Before he did anything else, he needed to get to Georgie and try and explain the storm that was about to hit and hopefully she wouldn't hate him for the rest of her natural life.

"Hello," Georgie croaked into the phone, still half asleep.

"Ah, hey Georgie," Millie said, "You, ah, you might want to turn on the television."

"What's? What?"

"Just do it," Millie said, "I'll stay on the line."

Georgie padded out of her bedroom and into the lounge, scrounging for the remote. She clicked the TV on and then waited.

"Okay, it's on, now what?"

"Channel seven," Millie said, her voice tremulous.

Georgie clicked over to channel seven and then sat with a thump on her couch as she stared at the photograph on the screen. It had been taken with a cell phone, but the quality was good and she could clearly see Connor sitting in a restaurant with a blonde. At first she didn't recognise the woman who sat opposite him staring at him with hearts in her eyes and then she gasped as she realised that the woman was her. She was the one looking at Connor across a candlelit table like he hung the moon and he was looking back at her with the same adoration.

"Shoot," she said softly.

"I think in this instance," Millie said in her ear, "You are allowed to use expletives."

"How did this happen?"

"Some idiot took a photo of the two of you and tipped off the media."

"Do they know who I am?"

"Not yet," Millie said, "they're just calling you the mystery woman. They have another photo too, one from when you went hiking."

"Damn it," she swore softly, "Marilyn."

"Apparently she put the photo on her blog and gushed about how nice Connor was to her. She didn't even mention you."

"Well thank god for small mercies," Georgie said. The phone buzzed in her hand and she heard a beep signally an incoming call. She pulled it away from her ear to look at the caller ID.

"I'll, ah, have to get back to you," she said to Millie, "My mother's calling."

She hung up from Millie and answered her mother's call hoping that it was only the monthly call that she usually got from her parents and not because her mother had seen the news.

"Georgiana," her mother said, her voice cool, "What nonsense is this? You're dating Connor Faulkes?"

Georgie sighed, surprised her mother even knew who Connor Faulkes was.

"We had one date," she said into the phone.

"It looks like more than one date from where I'm standing. How on earth did this happen?"

Her mother made it sound like she had released a reengineered version of the plague, not gone on a date with a celebrity.

"His grandmother is in my Book Club," Georgie said, trying hard to sound patient and calm. "Connor is visiting her, looking after her while she heals."

"He looks like he's taking more interest in you than in his grandmother," her mother said, her tone disapproving. "You need to put a stop to this nonsense. Your father and I are much too busy to deal with this and your gallivanting around with a movie star is going to cause all sorts of dramas that the lab can't afford."

"How is my dating Connor going to affect you?" Georgie asked, angry that her mother had once again made a situation all about her.

"Once your name is released you will be linked with me and

your father. The university will be overrun with press and the lab will come under media scrutiny. We can't afford any of this to disrupt the important work we are doing. You need to stop this, now."

"Are you serious?" Georgie asked, her anger bubbling over. "You don't give a damn about how this will affect me, just what it's going to mean to your life. Did you ever care about me or was I just some kind of experiment for you? When you decided to have a child was it because you wanted to build a family or because the scientist in you was curious to see what being an incubator felt like?"

Her mother was strangely quiet on the other end of the phone and Georgie felt it like a stab to the heart.

"Okay, then," she said, her voice strangely calm, "I suppose that's my answer. Thanks for your call Dr. Danners, don't bother calling again."

She hung up the phone and stood, shocked to the core at having her suspicions proven. Her parents had never loved her, had never really taken any interest in her except how she could make them look to their peers. Now that she had turned her back on the career they had wanted for her and was, in their eyes, a failure, they had no time for her. She should have expected it, should have known. Their complete lack of parental care should have been all the evidence she needed to see the truth. There was a side of her, however, that had always yearned for that perfect family and she'd held on to foolish hope that one day she might actually get it. That somehow her parents would show her they loved her and were proud of her. Instead, she was left with the realisation that she was nothing more than a social experiment gone wrong.

A sharp knock at the door made her jump.

"Georgie!" Connor called through the wood, "please let me in. I know you're probably really upset with me right about now, but please just let me explain."

She crossed the room and threw the door open, flinging herself into his arms and bursting into tears. His arms held her close as he manoeuvred them into the apartment and shut the door behind them.

"Hey," he said, brushing a kiss on the top of her head, "It's okay, I've got this."

She sniffed back her snobs, burrowing into his chest. "It's not that," she said, "it's my parents."

"Oh sweetheart," he said sitting down on the couch and pulling her into his lap, cradling her close. "What happened? Are they okay? Do you need to go to them?"

"I never want to see them again," she said, clutching at his shirt.

"Is it because of me? Did I do this?"

She looked up at him and saw the concern and regret in his eyes and she lifted her chin and brushed a kiss across his lips.

"No," she whispered, "It wasn't you."

He dipped his head and kissed her again and she let herself go, surrendering to his ministrations and letting him make her forget for just a little while that she was little more than a lab rat.

❧   11   ❧

Sometime later Georgie roused herself and smiled up at Connor.

"Thanks," she said.

"Anytime," he replied with a grin.

Georgie slid off his lap and stretched, realising she was only wearing her shortie pyjamas. Her face flushed. "Um, what time is it?"

"A little after nine, why?"

"Shoot," she said, "I have to get to work."

"Millie's down there," he said as he stood and stretched too, "I saw her when I came up."

She sighed. Her friends were too good to her. "It's supposed to be her day off, I really need to get down there."

"Okay," he said, shooting her a smile, "Can we have lunch today?"

She felt all soft and gooey as he looked at her. Life had been such a rollercoaster since last night that it felt like a week since they'd been on their date.

"Sure," she replied.

He brushed his lips softly across hers before saying goodbye.

She stood for a moment just soaking in the fact that Connor Faulkes had kissed her, not once, not even twice, but more than three times now. She only allowed herself a minute to bask in it before she reminded herself she had a business to run.

After a quick shower she breezed into the shop, a feeling of satisfaction filling her despite everything that had happened this morning. Having Connor in her life felt good, felt right, and she wasn't going to let anyone take that away from her.

"Well hello there," Millie said, "I did not expect to see you today."

Georgie gave her friend a quick hug. "Thanks for covering me," she said, "But I'm good, great actually." She looked around the shop that seemed to be full of small clusters of women. "You look busy."

Millie shrugged, "They're all just browsing," she said, "They are drinking coffee though, so at least we're making some money out of it."

Georgie took another look, her brow furrowed. "I don't recognise any of them. Is there some sort of convention in town that I didn't know about?"

"Huh," Millie said, looking around, "I didn't notice that they were all out-of-towners. Maybe there is something big happening in Armidale and they're just here on a day trip?"

"Maybe," Georgie replied distractedly, but she wasn't convinced that was it. She had a sneaking suspicion that something else was going on and she didn't like it, not one bit.

"Are you able to hang around for a bit or do you need to go?"

"I'm here for as long as you need me."

"Thanks, Millie."

They worked alongside one another for most of the morning, Georgie helping out in the cafe when she was needed. The little groups seemed to grow until the small shop was practically bursting with women who all seemed to be dressed in rather skimpy clothing for the middle of the day in the small sleepy town of Oxley Crossing. There were no beaches here or even a local swimming pool to warrant the plethora of nearly naked ladies that had descended on her shop. If they were just sitting around nursing one cup of coffee she might have gotten mad, but they were actually buying stuff so she couldn't in good conscience kick them out just because she didn't like what they were wearing.

By lunch time there were no free tables in the cafe and the noise of the conversation between the women was getting too loud for Georgie to think. She did not like crowds one bit. Part of the allure of owning a small book shop was that it was not a place for crowds to congregate, except that today, it seemed it was. She would be glad when Connor got here and she could take a break.

Oh God.

Georgie groaned and rolled her eyes. She was such an idiot. These women weren't here because they'd heard about her delicious espresso coffees or the homemade muffins. They weren't here because of her outstanding selection of books. They were here because of Connor. Somehow they'd found out that he came here and these women were all lying in wait for him. As if to prove her point, one woman, a tall, thin and stunning brunette, approached her.

"Is it true that Connor Faulkes is staying in town?"

"Um..."

She smiled cattily at Georgie, "That's what I thought," she said and then looked Georgie up and down, "You're the girl in the picture, aren't you? You're the one he's dating?" She laughed cruelly as she walked away and Georgie felt the stab as she always had when the girls at her school had picked on her. She was right, of course. It was laughable that Connor saw anything in her, especially when Georgie knew he could have any one of these women.

"What was that all about?" Millie asked, sidling up next to her.

"They're all here waiting for Connor," Georgie said with a resigned sigh.

"What, all of them?"

"Apparently so," Georgie said, "I should call him and warn him."

Millie nodded as she slipped down the back of the shop and into the little office. She pulled her phone out of her pocket and dialed Connor's number, but it went to voicemail. Next she tried Dawn.

"Hi Dawn, it's Georgie."

"Hello dear," she replied, "Is everything okay?"

Georgie sighed, "I was wondering if Connor was there. I tried his cell but it went straight to message bank."

"He just left. He said he was heading into town for lunch."

Georgie checked her watched and saw the time. "Okay, thanks. I'll try him again." She did not want to worry Dawn by telling her that there was a crowd of half-dressed women lying in wait for her grandson. She redialed Connor's number and heard it ring, only, she could hear it close by, not just through her phone.

THE PHONE in Connor's pocket rang as he opened the door to Georgie's shop. He was momentarily distracted by seeing her name flash on his screen and therefore did not notice the collective gasp of breath from the very crowded shop. The sudden silence made him look up even as his phone continued to ring. Every pair of eyes in the place were locked on him and he realised that he had made a mistake. He hadn't thought they would find him so quickly, so hadn't taken any precautions.

A small gasp from the back of the shop drew his eye and he saw Georgie, standing there with her phone in her hand, her eyes wide and horrified by the tableau. What a scene it must have been, almost like everyone was poised for a flash mob. He took a step towards Georgie and his movement broke the standoff. Before he knew it he was surrounded by flailing arms and raised voices as the women in the store all tried to get a piece of him. If it wasn't so terrifying, it would have been funny. Scenes from the old show 'The Monkeys' flashed through his head as he tried to hold the women at bay. Small fights were breaking out around him as they all jostled for position and he was helpless to do anything, fearing for the safety of his fans and for Georgie.

He tried to sign as many autographs as he could as people shoved pens in his hands and cameras in his face. Sure he'd dealt with a crowd of fans before, but he'd always had security to keep them back. He had lost count of the number of times his butt had been pinched and his arms squeezed and his cheek kissed. They were ravenous and desperate and not above hair pulling.

The sound of a bullhorn had everyone covering their ears and silence descended. He looked up to see Millie had climbed onto the counter and had the bullhorn raised in her arm like some sort of conquering warrior.

"Step back ladies," she said, "And I use the term loosely because you are all acting like a pack of hyenas. Give the man some space, would you?"

There was grumbling in the crowd and a renewed push towards him, but she squeezed the horn again, longer this time and the crowd once again stopped.

"If you do not do as you are told you will be forcefully ejected from the premises and banned for life."

"Yeah?" someone called form the crowd, "Are you going to do the ejecting?"

Millie smiled, "No, but they will," she said and pointed behind the crowd. Heads swivelled to see a couple of cops and a few burly looking men in a range of clothes from construction, fireman and local security to farmhand and mechanic. For a moment he was struck by the weird resemblance to the Village People, albeit an Australian version. The song YMCA started playing in his head as he watched the women step back from him giving him room to breathe. That was when he noticed the flashing cameras of the paparazzi and the news cameras all recording the mob. He looked around to try and find Georgie and caught Millie's eye. She shook her head in what he hoped was silent communication for 'she's not here' and not 'she doesn't want to see you'.

"Okay people!" Millie yelled, all eyes snapping to her, "We're going to do this nice and easy. You are going to line up in an orderly fashion and we are going to let Mr. Faulkes have a seat where he will be delighted to sign your autographs." The crowd started to move and pushing and shoving resumed. "If things get out of hand and you all can't act like ladies, I'll have these nice men escort you out without your autograph and your five seconds of Connor Faulkes, got it?"

The crowd settled and formed some semblance of a line while Connor was ushered to a table in the cafe and given a bottle of water. He grabbed Millie's arm before she could abandon him and pulled her down so he could talk to her without the whole shop overhearing.

"Where is she? Is she okay?"

"She's fine and she's hiding in her apartment upstairs."

He felt a moment of relief and then consternation. He wanted her here, where he could see her, where he could make sure she was okay with his own two eyes. But she'd rabbited like the scared little bunny she was, back into her hiddey hole and he wondered whether he'd ever be able to coax her out again. Their perfect little idyll, the cocoon that they had been in where the rest of the world couldn't interfere, had been invaded by fans and press. He just wanted more time with her, time to cement what had already been happening between them, to make it stronger to withstand the onslaught of what his real life was like. He could already feel the gossamer threads tearing under the pressure of what being with him would be like and he only wished that he had been able to keep it all at bay for just a little bit longer. But it didn't appear that he was going to get his wish.

$\mathcal{H}$ 1 2 $\mathcal{H}$

Georgie found herself sitting in stunned silence on her couch wondering what had just happened. Was Connor really downstairs being mobbed by women who had driven who knew how many kilometres just to see him? Was this his reality?

She huffed out a breath. Her life here in Oxley Crossing was quiet and undisturbed and she liked it that way. This was her real life. But it wasn't Connor's. Connor's real life was like a nightmare to her. Could he even walk down the street without attracting all that attention? How did he live his normal life?

She knew now they had been lucky. The town was obviously used to him being here and didn't get all star-struck and stupid when they saw him, but it was obviously not the norm for him. Those women down there had been rabid with no thought for life or limb in their attempt to get close to him.

He could have had any one of them with just a quirk of his lips.

Her breath whooshed out of her. They hadn't made any commitments to each other, but after last night and then this morning when he'd just held her as she cried, she felt like they were heading somewhere, somewhere she had never ever expected to go with him. But was that what he wanted or was she just a convenient body? Was their relationship built solely on proximity?

Looking down at herself in her jeans and t-shirt she huffed out a laugh. What had he ever seen in her anyway? She was nothing like those other women with their tiny little skirts and shorts and their mile-long legs. Never before had she felt so frumpy. She knew she was different and she mostly liked her own quirky style, but in the face of all that glamour she felt decidedly out-cast and those women weren't even the beautiful celebrities that Connor normally associated with.

Wow. He must have been really slumming it with her. She hadn't seen it before, hadn't really had anything to compare it with, but now, now it stood out in stark relief. She was a kitten compared to those cougars and cheetahs and panthers down there.

For the first time in her life she wished she was different. Georgie had always been content to march to her own drum. In her eyes, her differences had set her apart and she had leaned into them, not wanting to just be part of the herd. She strived to be her authentic self. She had never really fit anywhere, even with her own parents and instead of letting that eat away at her, she had let it build her up. She was an individual and she happily flaunted it. She had grown up in such a sterile environment where rules were meant to be followed and social conventions adhered to. What had started out as a way to defy her parents had morphed into something that she wore almost like an armour. The world was not a safe place for people who were different and she had set out to make her life as different as possible in protest. But now, now when her heart was on the line, she wished she hadn't been so ferociously independent.

Why hadn't she learned to wear heels and makeup and why

hadn't she taken more interest in fashion and hairstyles? If she had, she may have a chance to keep Connor.

Whoa. Was that what she wanted? Did she really want a real relationship with Connor? Even after seeing that mess down-stairs? Her head told her no, no she did not want that aggravation in her life. She did not want her privacy to be invaded and her picture to be taken by paparazzi and plastered all over the Inter-net. But her heart. Her heart told her something different. She was falling for Connor, and it wasn't just the childish crush she'd had on him for ages. Getting to know the *real* Connor had sparked something inside her. Her crush paled in comparison to her feelings towards him now and after seeing what happened today, it was scaring the bejeezus out of her. There was no way he could feel the same about her. It was inconceivable.

Her lips quirked up in a rueful smile at the line from 'The Princess Bride' but then they fell again. Her nerdy movie refer-ences and quirky shirts were just more reasons why Connor would never think about her the way she thought about him. They were far too different, living completely incompatible lives. There was no hope for them as a couple, even if Connor did return her feel-ings. Was he supposed to give up his life as a movie star to come and live in Oxley Crossing? Or would he expect her to give up her shop and follow him around the world? Whatever way she looked at it, someone always lost which only proved her point. There could be no Connor & Georgie - or Corgie as the entertainment media were bound to nickname them.

"Ugh!" Georgie yelled as she stood and shook herself out. She was driving herself crazy sitting here and making up scenarios that probably had no bearing on reality. She needed to distract herself.

Georgie grabbed her laptop and flipped open the lid intending to search for a new book to read. Her Facebook page was open and she had to look twice at the number of notifications she had. That couldn't possibly be right. Georgie clicked on the little icon and the list of mentions of her and posts on her page was ridiculous. And they all had to do with Connor.

How could this be happening so fast? She'd barely even come to terms with the fact that she'd gone out on a date with him and now the whole world knew and were commenting on it. The hashtag #connorandgeorgie was trending and there seemed to be a whole lot more photos of the two of them coming to light.

She slapped the lid of her laptop shut and escaped to her bed where she burrowed under the covers and determined that she would never leave the safety of her own apartment ever again.

MILLIE EVENTUALLY MANAGED to force everyone out of the shop and then closed and locked the doors. Women and teenagers still had their faces pressed up against the glass and Connor felt like he was in a giant fishbowl. It had never been this bad in the city or where he lived in the Northern Beaches. He supposed it was because seeing a celebrity in those places was a little more commonplace, unlike seeing one in a small country town like Oxley Crossing.

It didn't make it any easier to deal with, though. Of course he loved his fans, but being mobbed like that was unacceptable. Yes, he was an actor, but he was still a human being. Didn't he deserve the simple right of respect for personal space? The hoard of women in the book shop had pulled out pieces of his hair and scratched his arms. One over-enthusiastic fan had even torn his t-shirt in attempts to get him to bare his abs so she could have a photo and touch them. If a man had tried to do that to a woman, he would have been arrested on the spot, but these women thought it was their right.

He huffed out a sigh and dropped his head back, closing his eyes and trying to find his calm. Connor was a pretty easy going guy most of the time. He was very focused when he was working, but in his everyday life he took things in stride. Today had severely pushed his boundaries and he felt a little frayed around the edges. What he really needed was to see Georgie, to hold her in his arms and just be with her. They didn't even have to talk. Just being in her orbit was enough to calm him and restore his good mood.

"How you holding up, slugger?" Millie asked, sitting opposite him at the table.

"That was insane," he replied with a shake of his head, "I think I need to pay my security team more money if that's what they protect him from."

"Some of those women were crazy," Millie said, "I've never seen the like, not even at the annual Boxing Day sales. Seriously, those women were certifiable."

"Thanks for taking charge," he said, "You saved the day."

She blew on her nails and shined them on her shirt. "All in a day's work," she said with a grin for him.

"How'd you get all those guys here so fast?"

"I have four brothers," she said, "One's a cop, one's a fire-fighter, one has a mechanic shop and the other one works construction. I sent out an SOS, they gathered a few friends and voilà."

"Tell them thanks from me, please."

"Sure," she stood and stretched, "Now you need to go and rescue Georgie."

"Rescue her?"

"Yep," she said with a nod, "because she is going to be upstairs over-analysing what happened today and driving herself crazy with the fact that you're a big time movie star and she's just a girl in a book shop."

He ran his hands through his hair. "God, what a mess."

"Yep. So go and fix it."

"Right," he said, "And how do you propose I do that?"

"Just go to her, show her that all this doesn't mean anything to you."

"It doesn't," he said, "I need you to know that I don't go out of my way looking for this."

She smiled at him and for the first time he thought she might actually like him instead of just tolerate him for the sake of Georgie.

"I know," she said, "You impressed me today, so go and make it right with Georgie."

He stood from the chair and headed to the back of the shop, away from the prying eyes, and up the back staircase to Georgie's flat. He knocked on the door and waited, but he couldn't hear any sound coming inside, so he knocked again.

"Georgie," he said, "It's me, Connor. Can I come in?"

Still no sound and he wondered if maybe she had gotten in her car and just driven away from the chaos.

"Georgiana? Are you there?"

A thump was his answer and he waited to hear whether she would come and answer the door. When he didn't hear footsteps he knocked again.

"Come on Georgie, I know you're in there. Just let me in, I need to see you to make sure you're okay. I'm worried about you. Please let me in."

There was no answer from inside and he waited, hoping she would let him in. The longer he waited the more worried he became. He lifted his hand to knock again when the door opened and there she stood, her eyes a little wild and her face pale.

"Thank god," he said before pulling her into his chest and kissing her. She was stiff in his arms to start with, but when his lips met hers, she melted against him and relief rushed through him. He was worried that the melee below had frightened her away.

He backed her into her apartment, holding her close and kissing her mouth and her jaw and her neck. He kicked the door closed behind him and then just stood still, holding her to his chest and breathing her in. Her arms were around his waist and it just felt right to have her in his arms. It calmed him and the panic and anxiety he was feeling from first the crush of people and then from when she wouldn't open the door, was smoothed away by simply being in her presence.

She began to struggle, not violently, but letting him know she wanted to be free.

"Not yet," he said, his voice rough, "I just need to hold you a little bit longer."

She settled against him and the remaining tension in his shoulders and neck melted away. What would it be like to come home to this every night, to know that she would be here for him, that he could just hold her and let the stress of the day fade away? He'd never thought about getting married before. He always knew he would eventually, but he didn't think it would be for a long time yet. Now, though, standing here with Georgie in his arms, the rest of the world locked outside and just the two of them in this tiny little shoebox of an apartment, he imagined a life with her and it just felt... perfect.

"WHAT WAS THAT, CONNOR?" Georgie asked, pulling away from him and going to sit on the couch. He felt the loss of her and followed, sitting close beside her so that he could be near enough to touch her.

"That has never happened to me before," he said, "But then I've usually got security around me making sure it doesn't happen."

Her eyes roamed over him, getting wide when she noticed the rips in his shirt and the scratches on my arms.

"They did this to you?"

He nodded, looking down at himself.

"That's crazy," she said and he felt her pulling away, if not physically then emotionally.

He reached out to take her hand, his fingers weaving through hers, anchoring her to him.

"It scared you," he said.

"Well, yeah," she replied, "They were like a pack of wild animals."

"You know I'd never put you in any danger, right?" He needed her to understand that.

"That's not the point," she said, getting up and pulling her hand away from his. "Your whole life is crazy."

He stood too. "No," he said walking over to stand behind her, "My whole life is not like that. That's only a very small part of it."

"But you work all over the world. People line up for hours just to get a glimpse of you in real life. You date models and movie stars and women who are beautiful and graceful and—"

"Georgie," he said cutting her off, "I assure you it's nothing like that."

"Maybe not, but I know that your life is nothing like mine."

He wrapped his arms around her and pulled her back into his chest, resting his head on top of hers. "That doesn't mean we can't make this work," he said.

She relaxed into him for a moment and took a deep breath, but then stiffened and pulled away.

"What exactly do you mean by 'this'?"

"Us," he said, confused.

"There is no us, Connor."

He clenched his hands and ground his teeth together as he tried to rein in his shifting emotions.

"I disagree," he said, "There is something between us. Yes it's new and yes we're still discovering each other, but you can't tell me that there is no us."

She whirled on him, her eyes flashing. "There can't be an us," she said, "How would it even work? I can't leave Oxley Crossing and you can't walk away from your career. There's just no way for this to work."

He stepped into her personal space and wrapped his arms around her, dropping his mouth to hers in a searing kiss. When he lifted his head, the fire in her eyes had been replaced by something different and he knew she was feeling the same as him.

"I don't know the logistics," he said, not letting her out of his arms, "And I can't promise you it will be plain sailing from here on out. What I can tell you is that I am falling for you and I want us to work this out. I want you in my life Georgie."

Her eyes were saucers as she looked up at him. "You're falling for me?" The disbelief was plain in the hushed timbre of her voice.

"Yes," he said, his voice husky, "Please tell me you feel the same."

It was an odd feeling for him, the vulnerability that came with laying his feelings bare. Connor had never been afraid of anything. He didn't get nervous or anxious about new experiences. But telling a woman how much he cared for her when he wasn't sure that she felt the same? That was frightening the life out of him.

"I do," she said, resting her head on his chest, her words allowing him to breathe again. "But I still don't know how we are going to make it work."

"We don't have to figure it all out now," he said, "All we need to do is look at the next step. We'll take it day by day, but you have to promise me something," she looked up at him, "You have to promise me you won't run."

He saw the fear flash across her face, but he didn't let go of her and he kept his own face open allowing her to see into him, to see the truth of how he felt about her. He may not have yet said the 'L' word, but it swirled around them, a palpable presence in the air.

"Okay," she said softly.

He bent his head and kissed her sweetly, taking his time to memorise the way her lips felt under his. She was soft and sweet and fit in his arms like she was the missing piece in his life. When he came to Oxley Crossing to look after Gran, he never in a million years thought he would find the one person who could fill that hole in his life.

When he broke the kiss he could tell that Georgie was calmer, that the nervous energy that had been running through her before was gone. He knew he had to broach the next tough subject.

"So, what do you want me to tell the media?" he asked, and hated himself for the way she stiffened again.

"Why do we have to tell them anything?"

"If we say nothing then they are going to hound us and follow us around trying to find out what is going on."

"Surely we don't have to say anything now," she said.

He dropped his hands from her waist to her hands and pulled her towards the front windows that overlooked the street.

"Look," he said.

She looked out the window and gasped. Below them was a crowd of people. Some of them were women from earlier, but the majority of the crowd was paparazzi and reporters.

She stepped back, her face paling and her hand going to cover her mouth.

"Don't panic—"

"Don't tell me not to panic," she said, "I am being held hostage in my own home."

"I know it looks bad right now—"

"Connor there are cameras and microphones and talking heads down there just waiting to pounce as soon as one of us leaves the building. Please stop understating the situation."

"They just want a statement from me and then they will go away."

She scoffed.

"Okay, they might not leave straight away, but they will eventually as long as I give them something. So what is it going to be? Will I go out there and tell them you're my girlfriend or do I tell them we're just friends?"

"You want me to be your girlfriend?"

He rolled his eyes as he pulled her into another hug. "What do you think I've been saying for the last half an hour? I'm falling for you, I want you in my life. Yes, I want you to be my girlfriend."

She burrowed into his chest and he held her, letting her think through the next step and loving the fact that she wasn't pulling away, wasn't running, but was actually seeking comfort from him.

"I want to be your girlfriend," she murmured into his chest, "But I don't think I'm ready for the world to know."

"Okay," he said, sighing with relief, "okay."

❧ 13 ❧

Connor managed to escape from Georgie's apartment via the back stairs, giving the slip to the press camped out front. He knew he had to face them and he would, but not until his team was assembled. He was waiting on Ike, his head of security, and Tina, his public relations manager, to arrive before he spoke to the media. He didn't want to do a press conference, especially when there wasn't anything to tell. Georgie didn't want to go public with their burgeoning relationship and neither did he. Not because he didn't want the world to know about her and how he felt about her, but because he didn't want them and their big muddy feet to sully what was, at the moment, pure and beautiful. As soon as the press got involved, things were bound to change and the longer he could keep that from happening, the better.

A large black car with tinted windows was waiting in the driveway of his grandmother's house when he got home. He parked his truck on the street and headed into the house with a big grin. Ike met him at the door with a back-slapping man-hug.

"Sorry to ruin your vacation," Connor said to his friend. Ike had worked for him from the beginning, when his fame really started to impact his daily life. Connor had immediately liked him and they had become close friends.

"No problem," Ike replied, "I was getting sick of the peace and quiet anyway."

Ike was a big man with dark skin and islander heritage. He'd played rugby league in his younger days with a brief stint playing for the North Queensland Cowboys. Eventually the pressure had proved too much for him and after one too many drunk driving charges, he'd been dropped from the team. After some soul searching he'd found his way into personal security and had been working for Connor ever since. He was now a confirmed non-drinker who treated his body like a temple, which suited Connor to the ground. Ike was great company on some of his more adventurous pursuits and having him along soothed the worries of his management team.

"I hope this girl is worth all this trouble," Ike said as they walked into the kitchen.

"She is," Connor said with a grin, "She so is. I think she might be 'the one.'"

Ike looked at Connor with an unreadable expression. The other man had been there through all of Connor's previous failed relationships (not that Connor was all that prolific in the romance department). He was usually too busy working, which was why most of his relationships broke down.

"The one, huh?"

"I know it's early days," Connor said, "And I know there are going to be issues we have to sort out, but, yeah, I think Georgie is it for me."

After a moment of silence, Ike huffed out a breath, "Okay then. So what comes next?"

"I'm waiting for Tina to get here so we can decide on the best way to handle the fallout. Georgie doesn't want the world to know that we are in a relationship, so we'll have to come up with a story that will satisfy them."

"Sounds like a plan. When do I get to meet her?"

"I don't know, soon. It's probably best the she and I aren't seen together until the press decides there's no story and they leave. It really sucks, but it can be done. The mob that ambushed me today was scary and I'm worried about her safety as well as my own. Some of these women can get pretty aggressive and I'd hate for her to get mixed up in it, so I'll need you to look out for her too."

"Sure," Ike said, nodding.

"She comes here for a weekly Book Club meeting, which isn't until Wednesday. I'm hoping everything will be sorted by then."

"You only have another week here anyway," Ike added, "The press will most likely follow you when you leave."

"Yeah, I hope so."

A knock at the door interrupted them and Connor got up to answer it. Tina waited on the other side, a tiny woman with a bleach blonde pixie cut, sky high heels and tight leather pants.

"You do get yourself in some sticky situations when I'm not around to look after you," she said, foregoing the pleasantries to get down to business.

"I was being nice to a fan, I didn't think it would come back and bite me like this."

Tina walked into the house and down to the kitchen. Both she and Ike had been there only a few times before, but Tina never forgot a detail.

"Ike," she said with a nod to the big man.

"Tina," he replied.

"So give me the highlights."

"I met a girl. I like her. We're seeing each other. She doesn't want to tell anybody yet."

"A bit too late for that," Tina said, "The photos of you two out on a date have gone viral."

Connor grimaced.

"You're going to have to say something."

"I know," he said standing up and pacing. He ran his hand through his hair and wished that he'd never stopped to give that woman a photo. "I don't want to make a big deal out of it, is there some way to play it down?"

"Do you have something else to give them instead?"

"I start filming 'A Royal Engagement' in a couple of weeks."

Tina waved the suggestion away. "That's not enough. They already have your production schedule. You need to give them something new, something juicy."

Connor bit his lip wondering if it was too early to spill the beans about his new project.

"Spit it out," Tina said.

"I had a meeting with an independent film studio a couple of days ago. They want me to direct and produce a film with them."

"An Arthouse indie film?" Tina asked.

"Yeah, sort of. We want to get it into Cannes."

Tina nodded slowly, turning it over in her mind. "That's good," she said, "That might work."

"So what? We do a press conference and announce it?"

"Yes," she said, "and you say nothing about the girl. When we open up for questions they'll ask you about her and you just tell them she's an old friend of the family or something innocuous and then move on. Don't over-explain anything, don't give them any detail. If you want them to forget about her then you have to pretend like she means nothing to you."

Connor's gut clenched at her words, but he knew she was right. If the press got even a whiff of his feelings for Georgie, they wouldn't leave them alone. If he had any chance with Georgie then he had to get them to leave him alone.

THE PRESS CONFERENCE was set up for the next day. They decided to have it in front of the town hall - away from Georgie's shop. Tina didn't tell the media what the press conference was about and all assumed it would be for Connor to talk about his relationship status with the mystery blonde. Connor hadn't seen Georgie since the day before, but he'd spoken to her on the phone and told her what the plan was. She seemed okay with it. He also spoke to the Indie film studio he'd met with and they were happy for him to share the news of the upcoming project. Now all that was left to do was to feed himself to the hounds.

He wasn't nervous. Well, maybe a little nervous, but he knew what he had to say. He had memorised it and gone over possible questions with Tina in order to prep so his answers sounded believable. He wanted them to back off of him and Georgie and just give them some space to get to know one another properly without the pressure of it happening in front of the entire population of the planet, but he couldn't say that. If he even hinted that there was something between the two of them, the media would be all over it like a cheap suit.

Connor smiled as he looked out at the surprisingly large crowd of press who had gathered. When had his life become so interesting to others that it garnered this much of a response? Had he been hiding his head in the sand when it came to his fame or had he just been protected from it?

"Thank you all for coming," he began, "As you all know, I begin filming my new movie in a couple of weeks, which I have been really looking forward to. Following that, I have another new project in the works. I'm going to be working with a local independent film studio where I am going to have an opportunity to be on the other side of the camera and try my hand at directing. The project has been written by a young script writer who has had a small measure of success for her independent films here in the Northern Tablelands and I am excited to be part of this next one."

Connor went on to talk about the film and when he was done he opened the floor up to questions. As expected, nobody asked about his debut into directing.

"There has been a lot of speculation around the woman you've been seen spending time with. Is she your new love interest?"

Connor smiled but all the while his gut was churning. "I met the woman in question through my Grandmother," he said, "And she was nice enough to show me around so that I could check out some possible locations for shooting the new film."

"The two of you looked very cosy at dinner the other night."

Connor shrugged, using all of his acting ability to keep his face bland and his reactions hidden. "She's a very nice woman, but I hardly know her."

"Wasn't that her bookshop that you were in the other day when you signed autographs for your fans."

He nodded. "As I said, I met her through my grandmother who happens to be part of her Book Club. I went into the store to pick up a book for Gran who is laid up with a broken leg. The autograph signing was a spontaneous decision based on how many fans had turned out to see me."

"And what about the woman? Georgiana Danners is her name, isn't it?"

Connor hadn't known her full name was Georgiana... he liked it.

"I only know her as Georgie."

"So are you saying there is nothing going on between the two of you?"

Connor used his movie star smile on the reporter who flushed. "I hardly know the woman," he said, "We're barely friends, more just acquaintances. She was doing me a favour by showing me around, that's all there is to it."

"So will you be renewing your relationship with Laura Lovey when you start filming 'A Royal Engagement?' She is your co-star, isn't she?"

"Laura and I work well together and we are great friends. It will be great to see her again and get reacquainted."

"Does Georgie know about you and Laura?"

"As I said, Georgie and I are barely acquaintances."

"Will Laura be coming here to work on your indie film?"

"We haven't discussed it."

"But it's a possibility? She is Australia's favourite actress and the two of you together make your fans happy. We love seeing our two greatest exports together."

Connor's lips felt brittle and his smile felt forced, was forced. He and Laura had parted friends, but he didn't think she'd appreciate being dragged into this. She had moved on and, from what he knew, was seeing somebody else. He hoped this didn't cause issues for her as well.

"As I stated, I haven't spoken to Laura and I'm unsure whether her production schedule would have room for my new project. I do know our film doesn't have the budget for her. The plan is to use local talent and shine a light on what great, raw talent we have here, not only in the Northern Tablelands, but in Australia. I want to give young actors the chance to shine and that's what this film will be all about."

"Will you be seeing Georgie again after you leave here?"

"No," Connor said, although it broke his heart to do so, "There is nothing of consequence between us."

❋ 14 ❋

"There is nothing of consequence between us."

Those words cut through her like a hot knife through butter. She knew that she had told him to downplay what was going on between them, but to be so cut and dry about it? To completely deny that they were even friends? That hurt. And what was all that crap about Laura Lovey?

Georgie shut her laptop and lay back on her bed. She didn't know what to feel, but the overwhelming sense of being betrayed was foremost in her heart. He was just doing what she asked, but he did it so convincingly. Watching him tell the world entertainment media that she was 'nothing of consequence' hurt, hurt more than she thought it would.

When she asked him to keep their relationship a secret, she thought he might go with the 'old family friend' angle. At least then she could have had some importance in his life, but to be made out to be nothing but a local guide and friend of his grandmother was demoralising. Hearing him barely acknowledge her existence brought up all sorts of memories of the same thing happening to her when she was a kid.

Rejection stings, however you look at it and Georgie knew

that better than anyone. Her parents barely acknowledged her existence unless it was negatively impacting their own lives, and if her own parents couldn't love her, then how could someone like Connor Faulkes love her? It was the question that had plagued her all her life. Her parents were meant to love her just by virtue of being her parents, but if even they couldn't care for her, who could?

She had been a fool. Connor was an actor and she had fallen hook, line and sinker for his charms. The way he addressed the press, the confident way he spoke and the absolute clarity he used when he said that she was no one of consequence proved to her what she had been afraid of all along. Their relationship was just a distraction for him while he was here to look after his grandmother. He probably did this regularly. He probably chose the most unlikely girl and lavished his attentions on her and then just left. It was probably just a prank to him to see how quickly he could get some unsuspecting nerdy girl to fall in love with him. And she had fallen for it and fallen for him.

There was a pounding on her door, but she ignored it. She'd turned her phone off and had sequestered herself away from the crowds outside. She didn't want to see them, she didn't want to hear their opinions on her and Connor. Already the trolls had started tearing her down on social media. People she didn't even know we're passing judgment on who she was as a person simply by the way she was dressed in a couple of photographs taken out of context. There was no doubt that the fallout for her would be even worse after Connor's press conference. She could just imagine it now. They would say awful things about her, may even postulate that she had leaked the photos as a way to make out that she was his girlfriend.

Oh God. He had asked her to be his girlfriend and she had said yes. What a fool she'd been, what a naïve fool. He had only said it to keep her calm, she supposed. He certainly wouldn't want any bad press about how he led girls on only to skip town and leave them high and dry. He had the reputation of being a loveable rogue, a charmer, and he definitely wouldn't want that reputation ruined.

"Georgie! Let me in!"

Georgie rolled over and buried her face in her pillow, the tears falling hot on her cheeks. His voice. The way he said her name. It all hurt. He had completely destroyed her in the press conference, making her feel like she was unworthy of being in his presence. Making her feel stupid and awkward because she had fallen in love with him and she was 'nothing of consequence' to him. She couldn't face him, probably could never face him ever again.

He kept pounding on the door, but she refused to answer, refused to even acknowledge his presence. He would go away eventually. He was leaving town in a couple of days anyway and then she would never have to see him ever again.

That was probably for the best.

CONNOR COULDN'T UNDERSTAND why all the women in his life were mad at him. Georgie wasn't talking to him. In fact he didn't even know where she was and she wasn't answering her phone. Tina just shook her head whenever he looked at her. His Gran had thrown up her hands in disgust when he'd walked in and he even had a text from his sister calling him an idiot. Ike wasn't even on his side, shooting him disapproving glances from beneath heavy eyebrows.

"What?" he finally said into the stilted silence of Gran's kitchen. "I was only doing what she wanted."

"And doing it very convincingly," Tina said, "You and Georgie are no longer trending on Twitter—"

"And wasn't that the plan?"

"But you and Laura are."

Connor swore under his breath. Now Laura would hate him too.

"Oh, wait," Tina said, her eyes glued to her phone, "Now this is interesting."

"What?"

"Laura has posted something about the two of you—"

"She has? What did she say?"

"She's looking forward to getting reacquainted too."

Connor dropped his head in his hands and groaned. What did that mean?

"She goes on to say that it's still early days yet, but to watch this space."

"You've got to be kidding me."

"Nope."

"Get her on the phone. I need to talk to her."

Tina's phone rang in her hand and she raised an eyebrow at Connor.

"Jim," she said, "How are you?" ·

Jim was Laura's PR guy. Connor stood from the table and began pacing. He felt sure Laura would have had his hide for getting her mixed up in this nightmare, but for her to respond added fuel to the rumours already circulating about them.

He couldn't hear the other side of the conversation and Tina wasn't giving anything away, but she kept shooting thoughtful glances at him and he just knew that they were cooking up something between them.

"Okay, thanks Jim. I'll talk to him and let you know."

Tina disconnected from the call and sat, looking up at him, her face inscrutable.

"So?" He hated that she was drawing this out.

"That was Jim—" Connor rolled his eyes and made a hurry up movement with his hands. "Laura is dating a guy and wants to keep things on the down low so they were wondering if maybe a fake relationship might work in both your favours."

"Pretend to be dating Laura?"

Tina nodded, "Just to take the heat off. Be seen around the

place together a few times, you'll be working together anyway, so it would be easy to arrange."

Connor sat down, feeling like he had just opened Pandora's Box. He didn't want to pretend to be in a relationship with Laura, he wanted to be in a relationship with Georgie and he wanted the world to know it. But she hadn't wanted that; she was the one who had wanted to keep it quiet and now she wasn't even talking to him. How had things managed to get so screwed up?

"I don't know," he finally said, "I need to discuss it with Georgie first."

It felt disrespectful to even be considering it and he had to wonder what Laura's guy felt about it. Would the other man be happy seeing photos of Connor and Laura together and hearing speculation about a renewed romance? He didn't think so, he wouldn't be happy with that if the situation was reversed.

Without even talking to her, Connor knew Georgie would not be happy with this. If she wasn't talking to him over what had happened at the press conference, then she definitely wouldn't be happy with the rumours that he was back with Laura.

Connor shook his head. "You know what, Tina?" he said, "I'm not even going to ask Georgie because I know what her answer would be."

"So you're going to do it?"

"No," he replied, "I don't want the world to think I'm dating Laura. I don't want to hurt Georgie that way."

"You know the rumours are already out there and that you started them?"

He sighed heavily, "I know, but I don't want to feed them. If I can't be with Georgie then I don't want to be with anyone. Besides, the next few months are going to be crazy. The shooting schedule for the movie is insane and then I barely take a breath before I'm back here for the new project. I don't have time to have a fake relationship and a real one."

"Okay," Tina said, "I'll let Jim know."

She walked outside to make the call and Ike slapped a big hand on his shoulder.

"You're doing the right thing," he said.

"Thanks," Connor replied but he didn't feel any better for it.

If only Georgie would let him explain. He tried to do the right thing by her, he'd tried to do what she asked and he really didn't understand why she was mad. The best way to get the press off their backs was to totally shut down any speculation, which is what he'd done. Didn't she realise that? Couldn't she tell when he was acting?

He picked up his phone and tried calling her again but it went straight to message bank. He sent her a text, begging to see her, but he knew she wouldn't reply. Hadn't she promised not to run? But that was exactly what she was doing. He would wait a couple of days to let everything settle down and then he would go and see her and he would make sure she couldn't avoid him this time.

It was murder waiting the two days, but the last thing Connor wanted was to scare her away. If she needed time, then he would give her time, but not forever. And just because he didn't go and see her didn't mean that he left her alone entirely. He texted her several times a day, at first to explain why he was giving her space and then just to make sure she knew he was still interested in her. She didn't acknowledge his texts so he never knew if she even got them but it didn't stop him sending them.

He made Ike go and check on her, just to make sure she hadn't skipped town and that she was okay. The big man had struck up an easy friendship with her and with Millie, surprisingly. As far as he knew, the girls didn't know he worked for Connor or that they were friends, although he was pretty sure Millie had worked out the truth. He was pretty confident that if Georgie knew, she would have sent Ike packing.

In the interim he was kept busy running Gran around as they did final X-rays on her leg and then finally took the cast off. He'd organised a service to come in and clean and look after her for a couple of weeks until she was back to full health so that he didn't worry about her when he left. He also made plans for how to woo Georgie and make her see that everything he'd told her in private had been the truth, regardless of what had been said at the press conference.

He was making the final arrangements when his phone rang. He picked it up, puzzled by the number that was calling him.

"Connor Faulkes."

"Connor, it's Jerry."

"Oh hey Jerry."

Jerry was the producer on the 'Royal' movie. He had a string of box office hits and Connor had worked with him before.

"I'm really sorry to do this to you," he said, "But we need you on set, like, yesterday."

"I'm booked to fly in early next week."

"That's not soon enough. The studio is putting pressure on us to get it wrapped up and have shortened our filming schedule by two weeks which means if we don't get started now, we won't get it finished."

"There are lots of scenes without me in it," Connor replied, "surely you can shoot around me for a few days."

"We've done all we can," he said, "Laura has other commitments that we will be encroaching on if we push back filming. We really need you on a plane ASAP."

Connor sighed and ran a hand through his hair. "Fine," he said, "send me the details and I'll get there as soon as I can."

"You're a champ, man," Jerry said and then hung up. A short while later Connor's phone beeped with an incoming email. His flight had been booked and he was leaving first thing in the morning. He did not look forward to the twenty-plus hours on the flight but even more disappointing was that his plans for wooing Georgie would be thrown into chaos. He would have to try to see Georgie tonight and explain everything without all the wooing.

With his heart in his throat, he tried calling her. It went

straight to voicemail and he cursed under his breath. He got up from the table and grabbed his keys.

"I'm going into town," he called to his grandmother on the way past the sitting room and she waved goodbye to him.

He drove down the main street and parked right out the front of Bookish, sitting in his car for a moment psyching himself up. He didn't know how she would take his just turning up, but he had told her that he wouldn't stay away forever. He had a moment of panic thinking that he should have brought Ike with him, but the crowds and the press had cleared off after he had made a point of staying out of the public eye.

He took a breath and then headed inside. Millie was standing at the counter and her eyes narrowed and she shoved her hands on her hips when she saw him.

"It's about time you showed up," she said.

"I wanted to give her space," he replied.

"Well that was the wrong strategy. All Georgie has ever been given is space. She needed you to be there for her and prove to her that you weren't going anywhere."

"I'm here now," he said, "so where is she?"

"Gone."

"Gone? Gone where?"

"I don't think I should tell you."

"Come on Millie. I have to leave town tomorrow so if I don't see her today then I don't know when I will."

"Why are you leaving?"

"Something's come up with the movie and they need me there earlier than expected. I tried to get them to give a little more time. I had this whole plan worked out to woo her back but now I only have tonight so please, I'm desperate, where is she?"

"She's gone to stay with Kendra on the farm."

"Kendra lives on a farm?"

Millie nodded and then drew him a mud map giving him directions.

He ran to his car and immediately headed towards the outskirts of town. By the time he reached the farm, it was just on dusk.

He drove through the gates to Cooringah Downs Station and realised the 'farm' had been a misnomer. Cooringah Downs was no more a farm than he was a farmer.

The property was huge. The driveway alone was five kilometres and when he pulled up at the homestead, he had to stop and stare like a tourist. It was magnificent and huge and he felt decidedly underdressed. The place gave off an air of old time glamour and he expected to be met by a valet or a butler. But neither appeared, so he parked his truck and climbed out. The path to the house was lit with soft lights and the gardens that edged it were overflowing with native shrubs that were carefully trimmed so as not to impede passage.

He climbed the five stairs to the large wraparound veranda and knocked on the double wide door complete with lead-light inset. It took a while for the door to be opened but when it did, he was surprised to see Kendra.

She shrugged, "Millie texted me and told me you were coming. She's in the library."

Connor followed Kendra through the house, barely keeping himself from gaping at the splendour. How had he not known that Kendra was from Cooringah Downs? How had he not known that Cooringah Downs even existed?

Kendra opened a door and ushered him inside, closing it behind him and leaving him alone with Georgie. She looked up from the book she was reading and her face paled.

He walked towards her, determined to not let her get away from him before he had a chance to say what he needed to. He couldn't leave without her knowing just how he felt about her.

"Hey," he said, sitting down opposite her.

"Hey," she whispered, closing the book in her lap.

"You've been avoiding me," he said.

She looked down at her lap and shrugged. "I didn't think you wanted to see me."

"I've been texting and calling you," his frustration evident in his voice, "but you never replied."

"I've had my phone turned off."

"Georgie," he said, "Why did you run? You promised me you wouldn't."

"I heard what you said, Connor. I heard all about how I was 'of no consequence' to you. I heard about your co-star and how you were looking forward to getting 'reacquainted' with her."

"I only said those things because you wanted me to," he stood to pace. "I knew you wanted the press to back off, so I made it so they did. How can you be angry with me for that?"

"You made me sound like a nobody. You made me out to be of little value or interest to you. You couldn't have just said I was a friend? You had to take it one step further and tell them I was nothing to you?"

"I thought that was what you wanted," he replied, but she wasn't listening.

"And then there was that whole thing about Laura Lovey. You never once mentioned that you would be working with her in all the conversations we had about the movie. Don't you think I deserved to know that?"

"I didn't tell you because I didn't think it was a big deal, plus I thought you already knew—"

"But the thing that hurt the most was that you sounded so convincing, almost like everything you were saying was true. And that got me thinking—"

"I'm an actor, Georgie, that's what I do. I had to sell it, I had to make them believe—"

"But that's the thing, how do I know what is truth and what is acting? How do I know that the things you said to me were real?"

"How can you doubt us?" he asked going to his knees in front of her and taking her hands in his. "How can you take a few minutes of a press conference and let it wipe out everything that we shared?"

She was quiet while she searched his eyes and then her gaze dropped to their hands.

"I want to believe," she said, "But I've been hurt before and I... I just can't put myself through that again. You're leaving anyway, there was never going to be any future for us."

She pulled her hands from his and walked out of the room leaving him staring after her, wondering when the heck his life had gotten so out of control.

"Hey," Kendra said from the door of the guest room where Georgie had escaped to.

"Hey," Georgie replied despondently.

Kendra crossed the room and sat next to her on the bed, putting an arm around her.

"You okay?"

Georgie sniffed. "No."

"Oh, hun."

"I think I just did a stupid thing," Georgie said, the hot tears running down her cheeks.

"This is more than a crush, isn't it?"

"Oh God, Kendra. I'm in love with him and I just told him I didn't want anything to do with him."

"What he did was pretty low—"

"But it was what I wanted. I told him I didn't want anyone to know about us, he was just doing what I asked and then I got upset because he did it so convincingly."

Georgie cried silently. She had really messed up and had lost the only chance she would ever have of being with Connor all because of her insecurities.

"So what do you want to do?" Kendra asked, "How can we fix this?"

"I don't think we can," Georgie replied, "What kind of relationship could we have when I'm here and he's off making movies and hobnobbing with the rich and famous? I'm insecure enough now, but seeing him photographed with other women, more beautiful women, that would kill me."

"You're going to see that anyway, only now you have no claim over him. How are you going to deal with that?"

"I just won't look."

Kendra snorted. "You have been following Connor Faulkes' career for how long? You think you can just turn that off?"

"It will hurt too much."

"Why don't you go after him and try to fix this? He looked so dejected when he left, can't you at least try?"

Georgie wished she was different, she really did, but loving Connor, being in a relationship with him would take such a big shift in her thinking that she really didn't know if she could do it.

"I can't," she sniffed, "I want to, but I just can't."

Kendra stood and paced. "This is because of your parents, isn't it? Are you going to let their poor parenting choices ruin something that had all the hallmarks of being a real-life fairytale?"

"It would just hurt too much," Georgie said, "I can't risk getting my heart broken."

"And how is that different to what is happening now? You are already heart broken and you've only really known the guy a couple of weeks. At the moment you have all the pain without all the good stuff. If Connor wants to be with you, why can't you, just for a little while, suspend this belief you have that you're unlovable? Just for a few weeks or a few months? Just choose to believe him instead of what your head is telling you."

"You make it sound like I have a choice about the way I feel—"

"You do!" Kendra punctuated her remark with raised arms.

"It's easy for you. You grew up here in this beautiful place surrounded by family. You spent birthdays and Christmases and holidays surrounded by people who you love and who love you. You can't understand what it is like for me. My parents would rather be anywhere else but in the same locale as me."

"And that says way more about them than it does about you, can't you see that? I love you, Millie loves you, the whole freaking town loves you. Your parents were awful care givers and that's on them. Their actions are on their heads, not yours. Just because they were incapable of love doesn't make you unlovable."

"But what if it does?" Georgie whispered.

And that was her greatest fear. What if, after all was said and done, she was unlovable? For years she had been trying to tell herself all the things that Kendra was saying, that her parents were in the wrong and their behaviour had no bearing on who she was as a person. But what if her parents were right? What if she was a person not worthy of the love and attention of others?

Sure, logically when she looked at it with a rational mind, it sounded ridiculous. But deep down inside her where her core beliefs lived, there was a part of her that felt like she was unworthy of love and that core belief ruled her life. It was a hard thing to let go of. It was a belief that was so ingrained in her that it almost felt like she would never be free of it, which was a huge problem.

"Even if I went after him," she said to Kendra, "Even if I tried, this ugliness inside me would tear me apart. I would never trust his feelings for me, I would always be second guessing them or asking for validation of them. It would be a disaster for both of us. You can't base a relationship on a foundation that is so very broken."

"You just have to choose not believe those things about yourself," Kendra said.

"I don't think I can," Georgie replied, her voice hitching.

Kendra huffed out a breath, crossing her arms over her chest and nailing Georgie with a narrow-eyed glare.

"Fine," she said, "But for the record, I think you are making a huge mistake. You are letting your parents win again and losing the best thing that could have ever happened to you. That thing you tell yourself, that you aren't worthy of love? It's a lie that you are choosing to believe even when you know better. You may have had it rough growing up, but you are surrounded by people who care about you and you sitting there telling me I'm wrong to love you, that you are unlovable, that is disrespectful to me. I own my feelings, not you. I know you are scared to risk your heart on someone who seems so out of reach, but isn't it time you started to grow up and take some risks? He. Loves. You. You don't get to tell him he can't love you. You either choose to believe it and enjoy it for however long it lasts, or you choose to walk away and live in misery. But just remember, it is a choice and you're the one making it."

She turned on her heel and walked out of the room leaving Georgie to gape after her. She had never picked Kendra as someone who believed in love and to hear her say all those things was a bit of a wakeup call. Was she brave enough to trust in love?

$$\text{❦ 16 ❦}$$

He had been travelling for twenty-six hours straight. The distances he had to fly in order to pursue his movie career was the worst thing about living in Australia. Most of the time he didn't mind, it was the cost of following his dream, but this time was different. This time every mile he travelled took him further away from the woman he loved and that was worse than jet lag.

The car picked him up from the airport and drove him to his hotel. He had left Oxley Crossing at seven in the morning yesterday, so his body was telling him it was nine in the morning, but the local time was one in the morning. Of course the driver and the doorman and the concierge were all awake to greet him and make sure he was looked after, but it all seemed so... ridiculous. He was just a man and yet they went out of their way to make him comfortable. Of course it was their job and they were getting paid for it, but still. It was one o'clock in the freaking morning and here they were treating him like royalty. It was kind of ridiculous, or that could just be the jet lag talking.

Jerry wanted him on set at ten, which meant he had nine hours to sleep, except he couldn't sleep. He'd just spent twenty-six hours on a plane, the last thing he wanted to do was sleep. He flopped down on the large bed in his room and stared at the ceiling. He wondered what Georgie was doing. He wondered if she knew that he had left town. He wondered if she was still mad at him.

He picked up his phone and scrolled through the photos he'd taken of her. She hated being photographed so some of them had had to be done secretly. They were his favourites. The ones when she wasn't aware of her photo being taken and she hadn't stiffened up or tried to pose. He missed her so much. He missed her laugh and the sound of her voice. He missed the goofy t-shirts she wore and the way her hair glowed in the sunlight.

He wanted to call her, to try again to get her to understand how he felt about her, but he knew she wouldn't answer his call. How had it come to this? The job he loved meant that he couldn't be with the woman he loved. Was it asking too much to be allowed to have both?

With a grunt and a sigh, he rolled off the bed and headed for the shower. He was torturing himself with thoughts of Georgie. The best thing for him was to forget about her. He had pleaded his case and there was nothing more to do. She had turned him down, it was time to stop wallowing in self-pity and move on. He had a movie to shoot and then his pet project to plan. There was more than enough work for him to get lost in.

The hot water helped to clear his mind and he crawled back into bed. He did some deep breathing exercises to help him relax enough so that he could perhaps get a few hours of sleep. The upcoming day wasn't going to be too taxing, but he wanted to beat the jet lag as soon as he could. That meant forcing his body into observing the local time, which meant he needed to sleep even though he felt like it was the middle of the day.

He sent a quick text to Gran, letting her know that he had arrived. She would let the rest of the family know, not that they always kept up with his schedule. It wasn't that they didn't care, just that he had such a crazy life that he wasn't an easy person to track.

He groaned. His life was crazy and he spent more time abroad than he did in the house he owned in Sydney. He had been an idiot thinking he could have a normal, steady relationship with Georgie. He'd had hearts in his eyes and hadn't seen the reality like she did. The two of them lived in different worlds; she'd seen it and tried to tell him, but he'd only had eyes for her. Now that he was back at work, he saw the impossibility of it all. If his own family couldn't keep up with his schedule, what hope did Georgie have?

It was just another reason why he had to get her out of his head. She had been right, there were too many obstacles for them to even begin to have a relationship. All he had to do now was to forget her. Forget the few weeks of blissful happiness. Forget the way she felt in his arms and the way her body moulded to his when he kissed her. He had to forget how all that golden hair felt in his hands and the way she looked sitting in his truck. Yeah. He just had to forget all that and then he might not go crazy being so far away from her.

"WHATCHA LOOKING AT?" Millie asked coming up behind Georgie.

"Nothing," she said, slamming the lid of the laptop shut.

"Stalking Connor?"

Georgie blushed. "No."

"Liar," Millie said with a grin.

Georgie sighed and opened the laptop. "They've released some stills from the movie. Look at him in costume."

"Yowsa," Millie said, "He looks good as a royal."

Georgie closed the laptop again. "I'm an idiot, aren't I?"

Millie put her arm around Georgie. "No, honey, you're a survivor. You did what you needed to do to survive. I get it, I do.

Could you have made it work with him? Who's to say? Nothing is guaranteed in life, you know that."

"But I didn't really give us a chance. That's not surviving, that's being a coward."

"Maybe, but it's too late now."

Millie was right. It was too late. Connor had been gone for six weeks and in that time she hadn't heard a peep from him. After he left her at Cooringah Downs, she had turned on her phone and read all his messages and listened to all the voicemails he'd left and cried herself to sleep. She woke early, determined to make things right with him, but by the time she got back to town, he'd already left. She had vowed that if he called or texted her she would answer and at least open the lines of communication up again. But there had been nothing but dead air. Radio silence. She had resorted to cyber stalking him, soaking up every little bit of news she could find about him. It was pathetic but she couldn't stop.

"Do you have Book Club today?" Millie asked.

"Yeah," she replied.

Book Club was back in the shop now that Dawn's leg had healed, which suited Georgie just fine. Being in Dawn's house hurt too much; it was cloaked with memories of Connor. Not that her shop was much better since he had spent a lot of time there with her, but the memories weren't as poignant and there weren't photos of him scattered about like at Dawn's.

Georgie walked to the back of the store and began setting up the chairs. They had moved on from 'A Royal Engagement' and were on to a pick by one of the other ladies. 'The Second Chance Tea Shop' by Fay Keenan was bittersweet, but she just couldn't get into it. Not that she didn't like the book, it was more that she didn't want to read about other people finding their true love when she was recovering from a broken heart. She would much rather have read something a little grittier, a horror story perhaps.

Except that the Bookish Book Club only read romances, so she was stuck.

The ladies began arriving and Georgie forced her thoughts away from Connor and on to the job at hand. As hard as it was to focus, she knew it was imperative that she not give away just how upset she was. Dawn was like a bloodhound when it came to stuff like that and the last thing she wanted was for Connor's grandmother to know she was pining after him... even if she was.

Once the ladies had settled, each with the cup of either tea or coffee and a muffin, all eyes turned to Dawn.

"So," Maureen said, "Tell us what the latest is with Connor."

This was why Georgie hadn't abandoned Book Club. Every week for the last six weeks, Dawn had given them an update on where he was and what he was doing, even going so far as to read out snippets of his emails to them. Georgie unashamedly hung on every word. She was grateful that none of the Book Club ladies had questioned her about what had happened between herself and Connor, though the first week she received a lot of pitying and forlorn looks, which she tried hard to ignore. They knew there was more to the story that Connor had told the press. They had all witnessed the two of them 'courting,' for want of a better word. Thankfully no one had come outright and asked what happened and any queries regarding Connor were directed to Dawn.

"He's tired," Dawn said, looking at her. "The schedule has been gruelling as they try and get it in the can by the studio's deadline. Apparently Laura Lovey has a commitment that clashes with the shooting, so they're having to work around that too."

"The photos online look amazing," Kendra said.

The ladies turned to her. "There are photos online?"

She nodded. "The studio has released some stills of the characters in costume. It all looks beautiful and, well, lush. Just as you would expect a movie about royals would be."

"Connor sent me a photo," Dawn said, passing around her phone so everyone could see.

Georgie was the last one to get the phone and she stared down at the man that could have been hers and felt her heart break all over again. He was smiling at the camera wearing full formal regalia including the sash and star of his character's title. His dirty blonde hair had been darkened to match the description of Will that was in the book and it looked good on him. He was clean shaven and appropriately coiffed and Georgie hungered to touch him, to just be near him again, to hear his voice and have him smile at her.

A tear splashed onto the screen and she realised that she was crying. She sniffed and looked up. Every eye was on her and the faces surrounding her were arranged in pitying masks. She stood abruptly and shoved the phone in Dawn's hand, making her escape to the back office. She couldn't sit there and have them look at her like that. Their pity only drove home what an idiot she had been and she didn't need to see it, especially since she knew just what a fool she'd been.

❧ 17 ❧

Of all the things Dawn Hawkins was, stupid wasn't one of them. Nor was she oblivious to what was going on between Connor and Georgie. She knew her grandson and she knew he was hurting. She didn't know Georgie as well as she knew Connor, but anyone with a pair of eyes could see that she was also hurting. It made her mad to think of the two of them throwing away something that could be so precious over an obstacle that they could traverse if they just put their heads together.

While the other ladies tittered about what a mess Georgie was, Dawn put her thinking cap on. There had to be a way to get the two of them back together, but for that to happen they needed to at least be in the same hemisphere, the same time zone or preferably the same town. Connor still had a month of filming to do, but if they waited that long then there would be far too much baggage between them. Six weeks of this nonsense was long enough and if she could at least get them sitting opposite one another for a decent conversation, then maybe, just maybe they would be able to work out their differences.

She looked over at Kendra, the only Book Club member that

wasn't gossiping about Georgie and who was also giving her a narrow-eyed stare. That girl was far too observant for her own good. Dawn shot her a grin and Kendra raised an eyebrow in challenge. Taking a deep breath, Dawn stood, raised the back of her hand to her forehead and in a swoon worthy of Scarlet O'Hara, she fell to the ground in a faux faint.

"Oh my God," Kendra said, playing her part well. "Dawn, are you okay? Quick, someone get Georgie!"

The ladies all stood and gasped and Dawn lay still trying really hard not to smirk. She heard someone calling the ambulance and then Georgie was there, crouching over her, feeling for a pulse in her wrist and speaking softly to her.

"Dawn. Dawn. Can you hear me?"

"Connor?" she croaked, fluttering her eyes. It was a performance worthy of an Oscar nomination. Connor wasn't the only one in the family who could act. Dawn had done her fair share of treading the boards in local community theatre when she was younger. It wasn't a skill that was easily lost.

"Dawn, it's me Georgie," the poor girl said, cupping her face and trying to look into her eyes.

"Georgie? Where's Connor?"

"Oh, hun, he's overseas filming, remember?"

"He's not here?"

"You just hang tight," she said, "The ambulance will be here soon and they'll get you fixed right up."

"You'll let Connor know though?" she asked weakly, "He'll need to let the rest of the family—"

"Don't you worry about a thing," Kendra said, "Georgie will call Connor right now and we'll get someone from your family here as soon as possible."

"Thank you dear," she said, looking at Kendra who was shaking her head subtly in admiration.

She resisted the urge to wink at her and instead closed her eyes and waited for the paramedics. It was a cruel trick, but desperate times called for desperate measures. She knew Connor and she was confident that he would drop everything to come back and check on her. She didn't care that she was screwing with the shooting of his movie, his love life was more important.

The ladies fussed over her as she lay quietly until the paramedics arrived.

"How're you feeling Mrs. Hawkins?"

Dawn fluttered her eyes open and looked up at the man bending over her while the other paramedic put a blood pressure cuff on her arm.

"A bit light headed," she said, "And Daniel Wellington you know damned well I've asked you to call me Dawn."

He grinned down at her. "You sure sound like you're none too worse for wear, but we're going to take you in to the clinic just in case, okay?"

"Is that really necessary?" she asked, realising fainting might not have been the ideal thing to do.

"Yes, ma'am," he said as he helped her to sit and then stand. He supported her as he led her over to the gurney and helped her up onto it. She actually did feel a little lightheaded.

"Oh all right then," she said, lying back on the stretcher. "I'm sure I'm fine, though. I just got up a bit too quick."

"Be that as it may, my Gran would give me an earful if I didn't make sure I got you checked out."

"Your Gran is a good woman," Dawn said, "I wish she'd come to town more often."

"Her and Pops are living the life on the high seas and having a ball."

She smiled, "That's great."

"Now you just relax and let us take care of you."

Kendra stepped up beside the stretcher and touched her hand. "Are you sure you're all right?" she asked in a whisper.

Dawn patted her hand, "I'm fine. Just make sure Georgie calls

Connor. If I know my grandson he will be back here by tomorrow and then they can finally get this whole thing sorted out."

Kendra sighed. "I want to be you when I grow up," she said and Dawn winked at her.

"Hi Kendra," Daniel said and Dawn's antenna went up.

"Dan," Kendra replied coolly and then walked away.

Interesting, Dawn thought as they wheeled her out of the book shop and into the waiting ambulance.

GEORGIE HELD her phone in her hand and paced around her small office. She knew she had to call Connor. It was Dawn's wish that she let him know, but she had to psyche herself up to do so. She was both parts happy and terrified to speak to him. She looked at the time and did a quick calculation. It was two in the afternoon here and Geneva was eight hours behind so that meant it would be about six in the morning. Was that too early to call or did a family member fainting in her store circumvent social conventions with regards to the appropriate time to call?

Her vocabulary got real big when she was nervous, even in her brain, like she was trying to hide behind the five dollar words. She huffed out a breath and banged her head on the nearest wall. She could do this. She had to do this. Dawn needed her to do this.

That took the pressure off a bit. It wasn't like she was just calling him out of the blue for no rhyme or reason. Dawn had specifically asked her to call him, Dawn *needed* her to call him. This had nothing to do with their personal history, this was all about Dawn and what she needed right now. Okay. She could do this.

"Have you called him yet?"

Georgie jumped and spun around to face Kendra.

"Not yet," she said, "You do it."

Kendra held her hands up and backed away.

"No way, José," she said, "That's all you, babe."

"Okay," Georgie said with a resigned sigh, "Here goes."

She found Connor's name in her contacts and pressed the dial button, lifted it to her ear and then hung up before it had even started ringing.

"I can't do this," she said, feeling like she was going to hyperventilate or throw up or both.

"Yes, you can," Kendra said coming into the room and closing the door behind her. "The paramedics have taken Dawn to the clinic to be checked out. You need to let her family know what's going on and that means contacting Connor."

"Won't the clinic do that, though? Surely she has an emergency contact on file."

"It would be quicker for you to do it. Besides, she asked you."

Kendra had a point. It was her responsibility, not just as a friend to Dawn, but also as the proprietor of the business where Dawn collapsed. Of course she should be the one to contact the family. Which all sounded good in theory, but was a lot harder to action.

"Give me the phone," Kendra said.

"Why? What are you going to do?"

Kendra made a give-it-here motion with her hand and Georgie reluctantly handed the phone to her. She pressed a button on the screen and lifted it to her ear. Georgie could hear the phone ringing from where she stood and held on to a small glimpse of hope that Kendra might actually talk to Connor in her stead. Unfortunately that hope was dashed when she heard Connor's voice and Kendra held the phone out to her.

"Hello? Georgie?"

She rolled her eyes, of course he knew who it was. She took the phone and lifted it to her ear, the nerves in her stomach causing the option of throwing up a very real possibility.

"Connor?"

"Georgie? What going on, what's wrong?"

His voice sounded thick with sleep and she realised that maybe it had been too early to call.

"Sorry to wake you," she said, her voice tremulous, "But there was an incident with your grandmother."

"Gran? Is she all right? What happened?"

"Well, she, ah... she fainted in my shop."

"Oh God! Is she all right? Why did she faint? When did this happen?"

"It happened just a few moments ago. She was conscious and talking, but the paramedics wanted to take her into the clinic to get checked out just in case. She, ah... she asked me to call you so you could let the rest of the family know."

"Yeah, yeah, okay," he paused and she imagined him running a hand through his hair while he thought about what to do next. "Look, can I call you back? It's really early here and I just need to get my bearings."

"Of course," Georgie said, "I'll go to the clinic and see if I can find out what's happening. I'll keep my phone on and with me, so call whenever you need to."

"Thanks Georgie," he said, his voice less panicked and softer. "I mean it," he said, "Thank you. I'll be in touch."

The call was disconnected and she stood there looking down at it.

"What did he say?" Kendra asked.

"He's going to call me back. I think I might have woken him up."

"So we're going to the clinic?"

Georgie looked up and Kendra and nodded. "Do you mind driving me?"

"Come on," she said, grabbing Georgie's bag off the desk, "Let's go and check on Dawn."

$\maltese$ 18 $\maltese$

As quickly as he could arrange it, Connor was on a flight back to Australia, which wasn't all that quick. The flight didn't leave until nearly ten o'clock that night, so it still gave him a whole day of shooting. Jerry wasn't happy, but Connor didn't really care. They were just about done with his part anyway and he would be back in a couple of days. What was the use of being a big star if you couldn't throw your weight around sometimes? Besides, this was Gran and he was worried.

Seeing Georgie's name on his phone had been such a shock that he thought at first he was dreaming. He had been asleep, so it took him a moment to realise that it really was her. His heart had leapt into his throat with the thought that maybe she was calling because she missed him. He would have probably jumped on a plane to come and see her if she had.

Now he was doing the long haul flight, incommunicado for far too many hours and hoping that nothing went wrong with Gran in the meantime. He'd called Georgie back to get an update before he boarded, explaining that he would be arriving the next day. It had been three o'clock in the morning but she hadn't complained. Georgie told him that they wanted Gran to go in to hospital in Armidale for the night, just so they could keep an eye on her. She had refused, of course, so Georgie had stayed at her house with her to make sure everything was okay. She'd reassured him that Gran was fine, that he didn't need to rush home, but once he'd decided on the course of action, he had to follow through with it.

He had checked in again when they landed in Dubai. He had a four hour stopover and nothing to do but worry about what was happening back in Aus. Georgie had taken Dawn back to the clinic in the morning so the doctors could run more tests. He didn't get to hear the results before he had to get back on the plane.

If he was being honest with himself, Gran wasn't the only one he was rushing home to see. The fact that Georgie was talking to him again was another incentive. He could fly home, spend some time with Gran and maybe get a chance to speak to Georgie too. They may even finally be able to clear the air. The distance hadn't dulled his feelings for her as he'd hoped it would. If anything, those feelings were more acute now and knowing that he would be seeing her soon had his heart pumping and his hands sweating. Would she always have this effect on him?

The flight from Dubai to Sydney was uneventful and he slept as much of the way as possible. He had another plane change and a two hour delay in Sydney airport. He called Georgie as soon as he was through customs, desperate for news.

"They've admitted her to Armidale hospital," Georgie said, her voice husky from sleep. He had woken her up again, forgetting that it was still early in the morning. "They have some concerns about her heart."

Connor swore under his breath and ran his hand through his hair. He was glad he'd come home.

"Is she going to be all right?"

"I'm sure she will be fine. She was giving the doctor hell when I left, so I don't think you have anything to worry about."

"I've got another hour before my flight leaves and I will be landing at about twenty to ten. Ike will pick me up and I'll go straight to the hospital from the airport."

"Sure," she paused before saying, "Ike?"

Oh crap. He had forgotten that she didn't know Ike worked for him.

"So will you meet me there?"

"You don't need me there, Connor. Your parents are here and your brothers and sisters. In fact I think your entire extended family has descended on Oxley Crossing."

"I do need you there," he said, "I need to see you."

There was a pregnant silence, the phone line fairly crackling with unsaid things between them and then she sighed his name.

"Connor—"

"Please, Georgie. Please just say you will be there."

She huffed out a breath and he could imagine her squinting her eyes shut and crinkling her nose as she gave in to him.

"Okay, fine. I was planning on going in to see her anyway."

He grinned and for the first time since this whole drama started, he felt settled. She anchored him and knowing she would be there helped him to remain calm when he wanted to jump out of his skin in frustration at just how long it took to get home. It had been about forty hours by his approximation since she'd first called him to tell him about Gran and he had run the gamut of emotions for every single one of them.

"Okay, great. I will see you in a couple of hours."

He grabbed a cup of coffee and sat in the uncomfortable plastic chairs while he waited for his flight and the last leg of his journey. It was a good thing he liked air travel and if things went his way, he hoped to be doing a lot more of it. Coming home seemed like a second chance for him and Georgie, which felt uncharitable to think about when his grandmother was lying in hospital. He couldn't help it though and he knew Gran would want him to make the best of any opportunity he had to see

Georgie. His Gran had given him an earful before he left, telling him he was an idiot if he walked away from Georgie. He had been, but what other choice did he have when she refused to see him? Maybe the time away had been good for both of them, allowed them to have a clearer understanding of what they each wanted. For Connor, what he wanted had become crystal clear and now he just hoped that Georgie had had a change of heart. If not, he would have to convince her to give him a second chance.

She was standing outside the hospital when he arrived. He didn't wait for the car to come to a complete stop before he was out of it and rushing towards her. Without a second thought he scooped her up into a hug and breathed her in. God he missed her. Her initial resistance melted away as her body moulded to his and her arms snaked around his neck, holding tight to him. He loved that, loved the way she clung to him. He didn't want to let go, but a subtle cough behind him made him step back.

"Connor," his brother James said.

"Hey man," Connor said as he pulled him in for a hug. "Good to see you, how is she?"

James shot a curious look at Georgie before answering. "Gran is... well, Gran. She is raising hell and wants to be released, but the doctors are still running tests."

He noticed out of the corner of his eye that Georgie was inching away and he reached out and took her hand in his, weaving their fingers together and pulling her into his side.

"Have you met Georgie?"

James smiled. "We have met, yes."

He did not like the feeling that began to churn in his stomach. He had never been jealous of his brother before but if James had hit on Georgie then he was going to have to hit him.

James' grin widened as he saw the look on Connor's face and he slapped Connor on the back.

"Come on, let's go and see the old bat before she causes a riot." There was affection in James' voice. The whole Faulkes clan loved Gran, loved how outspoken she was and how she refused to conform to the expectations of a woman her age.

Georgie tried to tug her hand free, but he refused to let her go. If he had his way, he wasn't going to let her out of his sight, not until they got a chance to talk, not until he got a chance to tell her how he felt.

Georgie had been right when she said the whole extended family had arrived. Not only were all his immediate family in the little break room near the ward where Gran was, but his two uncles and their families were there too. It was quite a gathering and he knew that they would be getting kicked out soon if they weren't careful.

He hugged his mum and dad without letting go of Georgie, even though she gave it a good go. Then he man-hugged his other two brothers and then his sister, making sure that Georgie had been introduced to them. He went around the room, greeting the rest of the family and making sure they met Georgie as well. He was staking his claim, he knew, but he wanted them to know that he was serious about her and the best way to do that was to make sure she was by his side. He never introduced his girlfriends to his family because he had known that they weren't the women he was going to marry. Georgie was different.

"She's asking to see you, Connor," his mother said.

"Thanks," he replied, heading for the door, towing Georgie with him.

"Maybe you should see her on your own," Georgie said.

He stopped to look at her, searching her eyes. He did want to speak to Gran privately but he was afraid that given half the chance, Georgie would run again.

"I promise I'll wait for you," she said and she reached up to cup his jaw. He closed his eyes and leaned into her touch.

"Okay," he breathed.

James stepped up beside them. "I'll look after Georgie," he said with a wink, "You go and see Gran. She's been a nightmare asking for you every five minutes. I'm pretty sure that if you don't get in there soon, she will get out of bed and come find you."

"Okay," he said, squeezing Georgie's hand. "Promise you'll wait?"

"I'll make sure she doesn't go anywhere," James said and a silent communication passed between them

James had picked up on his feelings for Georgie and he was giving him the nod. He liked her and was happy for Connor and he would make sure she didn't run away while he was in with Gran.

Reluctantly he pulled his hand away and walked into the room where his grandmother lay, a scowl on her face.

"Took you long enough," she said as he bent over to kiss her cheek.

"It's good to see you too, Gran," he said, settling himself on a chair beside the bed. She was in a private room, thank goodness, so it gave them some privacy.

"If I had known all this was going to happen I wouldn't have done it," she mumbled under her breath.

"What?"

"Nothing," she said with a sharp shake of her head. "Now that you're here I just want to get out of this place."

"I don't think the doctors would have admitted you unless there was something wrong."

"But that's just it," she said, exasperated, "There isn't anything wrong, there never was."

"What?"

She waved the question away and shook her head. "These doctors are imbeciles. I'm fine, fit as a fiddle."

"No, Gran, you're not. You fainted and now they think there is something wrong with your heart."

"No, I didn't and there is nothing wrong with my heart."

"You are not making any sense," Connor said, shaking his head.

She sighed and patted his hand. "I didn't faint, not really. It was just a little ruse to get you and Georgie talking again. You were both so miserable and when she started crying in Book Club, I knew I needed to do something. So I pretended to faint. I did not think it would turn into this three-ringed circus!"

"Are you serious?" Connor stood and began pacing. "Do the doctors know you're faking it?"

She sighed and crossed her arms over her chest. "I told them when they tried to admit me the first time, but they insisted on running some tests. Then they apparently found something and so here I am being poked and prodded and held hostage until they can determine what it is they found."

"So there is actually something wrong?"

"Apparently," she said sounding most put out by it. "If I had known they would find something, I would have chosen a different tactic to get you and Georgie back together."

Connor didn't know how to feel. He was angry that she had pulled such a stunt, but the fact that they had actually found something made the stunt a little less idiotic and more fortuitous, especially if they caught whatever it was in time to fix it. He was also torn over her interference in his life. On one hand he was mad she had manipulated him, and on the other he was glad she had forced his hand.

"You are a menace," he said, sitting back down and taking her hand.

"But you love me," she said and he grinned.

"Of course I do. Now let's see what we need to do to get you out of here."

❧ 19 ❧

Things happened very quickly once Connor was back. The doctors came and spoke to him and Dawn and then she was released under the proviso that she came back in a couple of days so they could run a few follow-up tests. They had been concerned about an echo they had heard in her heart, and her cholesterol levels were too high. The doctors put her on medication and wanted to monitor her until they were sure she was out of danger.

Georgie had tried to leave, but the Hawkes and Faulkes clans would have none of it. Somehow they had gotten the message that Connor wanted her to stay, so they made sure she stayed. It wasn't really a hardship. They were all lovely and Connor's sister Amelia (who was hugely pregnant at this point) had stuck close to her side. Georgie was surprised to discover that they had a lot in common and seemed to have similar tastes in books and movies. Georgie could almost admit that Amelia was as much of a nerd as she was and it was a big surprise. Who'd have thought that Connor Faulkes had a nerdy sister?

When Connor came back into the waiting room, his eyes immediately sought her out and he seemed to relax when he saw her. He made a beeline for her and she stood to meet him. He wove his fingers through hers as he turned to fill the family in on what was happening. He seemed to need the connection with her and if she was honest with herself, she needed it too.

Georgie had been petrified about seeing Connor again, but he hadn't made it awkward at all and she was grateful. It was almost like their last fight hadn't happened and she was lulled into thinking they could go on pretending that it hadn't. That wasn't real life though, and they would have to talk but for right now, she was just happy to be in his orbit once again.

Most of the family left after Connor told them Dawn would be released imminently. They went back to the house to prepare for Dawn's arrival. They would all stay through the weekend and be there for her checkup next week. Georgie had to marvel at the family's obvious love for their matriarch. She had never experienced the solidarity and support of a family group and it made her wish she was a part of it for real and not just an observer.

Connor's brother stayed to drive Dawn home and when the waiting room was empty, Connor turned to her and she held her breath.

"We need to talk," he said and she nodded, unable to speak. "Come for a drive with me?"

She nodded again and let him lead her out of the hospital and into the waiting car. It was then that she noticed Ike in the driver's seat. He grinned sheepishly at her.

"Hi Georgie," he said.

"Hello Ike. I didn't know you knew Connor."

"He works for me," Connor said unapologetically and it all fell into place for Georgie. For that week when she thought Connor was avoiding her, he actually had Ike looking out for her. She should probably be mad about it, but she actually felt her heart warm. He had cared enough about her to want someone to keep an eye on her. No one had ever done that for her before.

Connor ushered her into the car.

"Where are we going?"

"To your place," Connor said.

They drove in silence, Connor sitting beside her, holding her hand. It was surreal and she had to keep reminding herself that it was actually happening and not one of her dreams. Her dreams had been filled with images of Connor coming back to claim her and although she didn't know if that's what this was, a girl could hope.

Ike let them off in front of her apartment and Georgie led Connor inside. She had only just closed the door when he pulled her into his arms and dusted his lips across hers in a sweet kiss. She sighed and let herself melt against his hard chest.

"Georgie," he whispered against her lips, "I have missed you so much."

She looked up at him and saw the sincerity in his eyes and she closed hers and burrowed into his shoulder, her arms squeezing his waist. They stood like that, just soaking each other in for a long moment before Georgie pulled away.

"Do you want something to eat or drink?"

He shook his head.

"I need to—"

"I missed you—"

They both spoke at the same time and stopped to grin at each other.

"You go first," Georgie said and then shook her head, "No, let me go first." He nodded and she took a deep breath. "I need to apologise," she said, "Those things I said to you were unfair. I have a problem believing that anyone could ever love me, but Kendra showed me how stupid that belief is. I blame my parents and the way they brought me up, but that doesn't mean I have to continue to let it affect my life. I was scared and I reacted badly and I'm sorry because the truth is," she paused to gather her courage, "I was falling in love with you and I didn't know how to do that. I didn't know how to be with you when you seemed so far out of my league."

"Was? Are you saying you're not anymore?"

Her stomach flipped over and her skin buzzed with nerves. "I was falling in love with you," she said quietly, "but I am now in love with you. Present tense."

He closed the gap between her and crashed his lips down on hers. "I love you Georgie Danners," he said between kisses, "And I am going to spend the rest of my life showing you exactly what it means to be loved."

GEORGIE'S HEAD was spinning with the speed by which Connor made things happen. Dawn had been released from hospital and had been given the all clear with instructions to take both her cholesterol and blood pressure medication and commit to regular checkups. Once Dawn had returned home, Connor practically swept her off her feet. He secured both Millie and Kendra's help and before she even knew what was happening, she was on a plane sitting in first class with Connor and on her way to Switzerland. Connor's movie was being filmed in Geneva on the shores of Lake Geneva, which was where the fictional country of Merveille was set.

"I still can't believe I'm here," she said, turning to Connor. "I've never been out of the country before."

"Lucky you had a passport or my whole grand gesture could have fallen flat." He leaned over and kissed her and she sighed.

"I always liked the idea of travelling, but never had the guts to go on my own."

"Now you don't have to worry about that," he said with a smile, and then turned serious. "You do know that I am in this for the long haul, don't you? You are not just a fling or a distraction or someone to have fun with. I am in love with you Georgiana Danners, I need you to not just know that but understand it."

Georgie felt tears burn the back of her eyes as she looked at the sincerity on Connor's face.

"I do," she said, "I know. I didn't before, I didn't understand, but I know now that you're not like my parents. And I also know because I love you and my heart beats with yours. I don't think that would happen otherwise."

Georgie kissed him this time just to show him that she meant every word she said. She had never expected to fall in love and had wondered whether she was even capable of it, but loving Connor came as naturally to her as breathing.

For the first time in her life she felt secure; secure in the love of someone else. She had never felt that way with her parents, had never been loved simply for being who she was. Her parents had only ever showed affection when she had pleased them and when they were unhappy with her, they had withdrawn that affection. But the way Connor loved her was different. She had really only known him for a few weeks, but she already knew that it was different, that it was more.

"So," Connor said after they were in the air and had settled in for the first leg of the journey. "After I have finished filming here in Geneva, I have a couple of weeks free before I start the new project. What do you want to do, where do you want to go?"

Georgie looked at him blankly. "What about the shop?"

He smiled. "Relax. I'm not going to kidnap you forever, just a couple of weeks. Kendra and Millie have offered to look after the shop and even Gran said she would help out. How long has it been since you had a holiday?"

"Not since I opened Bookish," she said and then bit her lip. "Are you sure they don't mind?"

"Positive. In fact it was Millie's idea. So where do you want to go?"

"Paris," she said, "I know it's cliché, but I've always wanted to go."

"Then we'll go."

"Have you been before?"

"I have, but never with the person I'm in love with," he squeezed her hand. "So it will be a totally new experience for me too."

She liked that he was always touching her. He held her hand or put his hand on the small of her back. He always stood close as if to reassure himself that she was there. She'd never been a touchy feely person but with Connor, she was a convert.

"And where will you go after that?" she asked, "I mean, where is your new project?"

"Armidale," he replied with a grin, "Which means I will be moving to Oxley Crossing. We intend to film in the Northern Tablelands and the studio is in Armidale for all the post production stuff."

"And then?"

He shifted in his seat so he was facing her. "Georgie," he said, cupping her cheek. "I'm moving to Oxley Crossing to be with you. Yes, I work all over the world, but I always have a home base. Up until now it was in Sydney, but now it will be with you. When I travel for work, you can come with me if you can spare the time. I don't want to interrupt your life or your business, but I figure we can find a compromise. I am committed to making this relationship work. And another thing," he said, his eyes boring into hers, "I don't want any misunderstandings this time. We are going to go public with our relationship. I want the world to know that I fell for the girl in the bookshop with the quirky t-shirts and the cute smile."

She blushed and he kissed her. "Okay," she whispered, no longer worried about what the Internet might say about her. She trusted Connor, believed he loved her and was committed to him too. The rest of the female population could eat their hearts out. She'd won Prince Charming fair and square and she wasn't going to let him go.

EPILOGUE

Six months later

They were well into the filming the first film that he would direct and the daily rushes were more than he could have hoped for. He couldn't wait to see the finished product and there was a lot of hype surrounding it, which was both exciting and scary. It could be a major flop, but he was willing to take that chance.

Tonight was the premiere of 'A Royal Engagement' and he and Georgie were heading to Sydney to walk the red carpet for the release. Georgie was nervous, but Kendra and Millie were with her, keeping her calm and helping her get ready. He'd hired a private jet to fly them to the city where they'd go straight from the airport to the theatre. They would then spend the night in one of Sydney's premiere hotels in the penthouse suite.

Connor pushed back from the desk where he had been watching the latest scenes from the day's filming and stretched. He checked his watch and stood. The girls were probably frantic that he hadn't arrived yet, but he wasn't concerned. He took about five minutes to shower and dress and he had plenty of time.

Being with Georgie over the last few months had been everything and more than he'd expected. It hadn't all been smooth sailing, but what relationship was? Everyday they both made the choice to love one another and that made it easier. When they were both committed to making it work, then the issues that came up never seemed insurmountable.

He drove home to the house he had bought only a couple of months ago. He had been living with Dawn when he first moved to Oxley Crossing, but when Singleton House had come onto the market, he knew he had to buy it. It was a beautiful old house that had been lovingly restored and had huge, landscaped gardens. Georgie had fallen in love with it when they went to look at it and that sealed the deal for him. If all went well tonight, she would be moving in with him in the not too distant future.

He walked through the door and the vision in front of him took his breath away. The girls were using his house to help Georgie get ready because there was a lot more room, and they would leave straight from there to the airport. He knew she would look beautiful whatever she wore, but the designer dress Kendra had found for her was stunning. It was a floor length ball gown (in keeping with the 'royal' theme of the movie) in a dark blue and studded with shimmering crystals. It looked like she had wrapped herself in the night sky. The sweetheart neckline showed off her creamy shoulders, and her blonde hair was twisted in an updo and pinned with crystals as well. He had no words.

"Wow," he breathed.

"Hurry up and get dressed," Millie ordered, "you can gawk later, we're on a schedule here."

He brushed a kiss on Georgie's cheek before he ran up the stairs to his room. He showered, shaved, and dressed in a tuxedo smiling, when he saw that Kendra had gotten him a tie to match colour to Georgie's dress.

News of his and Georgie's relationship had initially broken the Internet for a few days, but it had settled down. He knew that tonight would stir it all up again, but he didn't care. He wanted the world to know they were still together and going strong.

Millie and Kendra took some photos of them before he ushered Georgie into the limousine he had hired. Two hours later, after landing in Sydney, they were sitting in another limousine and pulling up to the red carpet. Georgie gripped his hand and he brushed another kiss on her cheek before getting out.

He was momentarily blinded by the camera flashes, but he smiled and waved anyway. He let the reporters get their photos before turning and holding his hand out to Georgie. He helped her out of the car to another round of flashes as the paps went crazy for her. They stood together, arm in arm for a moment letting the media have their moment and then he escorted her down the carpet towards the entrance. They were stopped along the way for the obligatory interviews and he was proud to say that, despite her nerves, Georgie charmed the entertainment reporters. He knew that she would, she just had to get over her nerves.

As they watched the movie, Georgie quietly gave him her critique throughout (which he loved). They then attended the after party, but didn't stay long. He hoped that everything had been set up to his specifications in their hotel penthouse, and for the first time that evening he was nervous. Georgie was quiet as they took the lift to the top floor and then gasped when he opened the door to their suite.

The lights were low and a trail of rose petals led from the door to the balcony that overlooked the Opera House and the Sydney Harbour Bridge.

"This is amazing," she said, turning around and taking it all in.

A bottle of champagne was chilling in an ice bucket and soft music played. They walked out to the balcony . While she was gazing out at the view he got down on one knee.

"Georgie," he said and she turned, her eyes dropping to him

and a hand covering her mouth. He took her other hand in his and smiled up at her.

"I had a whole speech prepared," he said, "but looking up at you now, none of it seems relevant. My heart beats for you and I don't know how I would survive this life without you in it. I love you with every breath I take and I want to spend however long I have left on earth with you. Will you marry me?"

Her eyes brimmed with tears that began to run down her cheeks, but she didn't say anything. For what seemed like an eternity, he thought that she was going to say no. Then she moved her hand and he saw her smile. He stood and pulled the ring out of his pocket, a stunning square cut diamond set in a platinum band, and slid it on her finger.

"Oh Connor," she breathed, "It's beautiful."

"So is that a yes?"

She giggled. "Yes. It's a yes."

She threw her arms around him and he kissed her and everything was perfect. Whatever came at them from now until the end of their lives, they would face it together and he couldn't think of a better person to do life with.

The End

WANT to know when the next book in the Bookish Book Club series is available? Go to Emma's website (www.emmaleaauthor.com) and sign up for her Newsletter.

KEEP READING for a sneak peek at 'Meeting the Wizard of Oz' the next book in the Bookish Book Club series

Kit Alexander, better known as The Wizard of Oz, was an international football star. He may have hit a bad patch there for a while, but he was clawing his way back to the top, right up until an injury benched him. With three weeks to kill and an invitation to a wedding Down Under, Kit's plans were on hold. he needed to keep his head down and let his body heal before they'd let him back on the pitch and that's exactly what he intended to do.

Being invited to the hottest wedding of the season was a dram come true for Charlotte Fox. She'd never left her small town of Oxley Crossing in the twenty-eight years she'd lived there–doctor's visits and hospital stays didn't count. Now that she was out on her own for the first time in her life, she was determined to store up enough experiences and memories to last another twenty-eight years.

A chance meeting in a bar late one night brought the two of them together. Kit would be leaving to go back to UK and his career, and Charlie was only in the city for the wedding and a brief holiday before she had to go back to her life in Oxley Crossing. It was only meant to be a flirtation, a holiday fling, nothing serious. But it's all fun and games until someone falls in love.

MEETING THE WIZARD OF OZ

is available now

CHAPTER 1

The Wizard of Oz. It was a stupid nickname but Kit Alexander hadn't always hated it. When they first dubbed him The Wizard, he felt like he'd finally made it. The boy from Australia with a boot that saved a Premier League game and a club from relegation. It was in his fifth year playing for Twickenham South Football Club—TWS FC—and Kit had been mostly unnoticed until the goal that earned him the nickname and the celebrity that went with it. That was ten years ago and he'd been traded several times in the intervening years until an unfortunate on-field injury and an even more unfortunate off-field incident made him persona non-grata with the big name clubs. Now he was back at TWS and back in the news—for positive reasons this time. Kit was in form and the old nickname had resurfaced. TWS weren't going to win the Premier League, but at least they weren't going to crash and burn either, which was one of the reasons he'd been afforded the time off to come back to Australia to attend Connor Faulkes' wedding—the other reason was the minor injury he was carrying.

Kit flicked off the hotel television and tipped his head back against the seat. He knew he shouldn't watch the sports news, it messed with his head. It didn't matter if what they were saying was good or bad, both affected him. It was too easy to let himself get cocky when he was a media darling—that's what got him in trouble last time—and if they were sledging him, that was even worse. He got more arrogant, if that was possible. The need to prove himself and prove the critics wrong made him stupid.

He tossed the remote and stood, rubbing his hands through his hair. Jet lag was killing him. He didn't even know what time it was. It felt like the middle of the day but the dark sky outside his window told him something different. He needed to get out of the hotel, get the blood flowing, have something to eat and a drink, and then maybe he would be able to sleep.

He crossed the room to the bedroom and flicked the light on in the ensuite. He splashed some water on his face and pulled his long, unruly hair back into a man-bun. He needed a shave and a few hours sleep before the wedding tomorrow, but now that he'd thought about food, he was hungry.

Kit tucked his hotel keycard into his pocket and tugged the door closed behind him. He hadn't been back to Australia in too many years to count. When he'd been selected for the TWS training academy, his mum and dad had sold up and moved to the UK with him. It helped that he was an only child and his mum's family were English. After seventeen years, the UK felt more like home than the country of his birth. Kit had lived overseas longer than he'd lived in Australia, but he would always be Australian, even if his accent made him sound like a tourist.

He took the elevator to the lobby and stepped out into the large open space. It was deserted except for a few staff. His watch told him that it was later than he thought which only made the jet lag seem so much worse. The hotel bar was closing, so he redirected his steps and headed out into the night. It was Friday night in Sydney, surely he could find something to do until he felt tired enough to sleep.

It was a short walk past the historic buildings that typified

The Rocks to the Orient Hotel. Live music blasted from the door as Kit pushed through into the crowded pub. He forced his way through the mob to the bar and ordered a beer before turning around to find a seat.

If he'd been anywhere in London, his face would have been immediately recognisable, but here in Sydney he was just another pub patron out on a Friday night, albeit alone. That was fine, he didn't mind being alone. He wasn't any good at relationships anyway. His last girlfriend, Summer, could testify to that.

He slid onto an empty stool and sipped his drink. The band was good and he didn't mind being anonymous amongst the Friday night revellers. He leaned back against the corner and people-watched, not something he got to do often. Fame had its perks but it also had plenty of drawbacks to balance it out. Going to a pub on a Friday night back home would result in speculation in the morning's newspaper about who he spoke to, how much he drank, and the impact his consumption of alcohol would have on the team's chances at the next game.

He loved football, had done since the moment he learned to kick a ball in the backyard with his dad. The fact he had the talent to support his love of the game gave him opportunities few people enjoyed and enough money to live the life of fairy tales and Hollywood movies. And when everything threatened to come crashing down on him, it was his love of the game that brought him back from the brink. He didn't have many years left as a player and he honestly didn't know what he would do when the time finally came for him to retire. It felt like he'd only just gotten his game back and he wasn't ready to even think about a life without it.

The band took a break and he noticed a game playing on the television in the corner. It was a replay of last week's game when TWS beat Tottenham. It was a good game and he'd come away with a goal. He'd also come away with a strain and the reason he'd been released to travel to Sydney for the wedding. The doctors wanted him to rest for the next few weeks because they wanted him for the last game. He didn't mind the break. It was good to get away from the craziness and refocus. He still had to prove himself to the team who'd taken him back when no one else wanted him. A trip back to Australia to celebrate with a friend out of the spotlight that was the English press, was exactly what he needed.

CHARLOTTE FOX STOOD underneath the Sydney Harbour Bridge, held her arms out wide, and twirled around, her head tipped back and her red curls fanning out around her. It was ridiculous and corny and she really should be tucked up in bed like the other members of her book club, but she couldn't sleep. It was her first time in the city and there was so much to see and do, and she wanted to see and do it all. She was the clichéd country mouse in the city, but she didn't care. This was her big adventure, the only one she was probably ever going to have, and she was determined to live every moment of it. She could sleep when she was dead...or at least on the flight back to Oxley Crossing.

Connor and Georgie's wedding had given her the perfect excuse to escape her real life and have a real life adventure. Amelia, the character in the stories she wrote, was bold and brave and always going on quests and attempting daring exploits, just like Charlie wished she could. Now she had a chance to experience just a tiny sliver of what Amelia did and she wasn't going to miss it by sleeping.

No one knew she was a writer. To all her friends and her family—her mother especially—she worked as a teller in the local bank. Which she did, but at night and on the weekends she spent her time writing about her intrepid heroine, Amelia, who saved the world on more than one occasion with little more than a hairpin, her quick wit and smarts, and her faithful furry sidekick, Mr. Chippers, an incredibly astute guinea pig. Amelia was the Kim

Possible of the young adult literary world. Amelia was who Charlie wanted to be.

She took a deep breath of the city air and coughed with the fumes from the traffic passing overhead. It didn't spoil the moment, she didn't think anything could. She took one more selfie and then headed for the next point on her bucket list—a live band. Earlier in the night she'd had dinner with the book club girls at Matt Moran's restaurant, Aria. Then they'd crossed the harbour on a ferry and gone to Luna Park. The older members of book club had called it a night then, but Millie, Kendra, Georgie, and Charlie headed back over to Pancakes at The Rocks. After stuffing themselves full with too many stacks, Georgie and her bridesmaids waved goodnight, but Charlie wasn't ready to go. It was Friday night in the city and she wanted to do something. She didn't know what, she just knew she wasn't ready for it to be over.

Charlie was no stranger to historic buildings. Oxley Crossing and the Northern Tablelands had their fair share of historic build-ings and the history to go with it, but The Rocks was something special. She could almost hear the ghosts of the past whisper to her as she walked along streets that had been there for over two hundred years.

She heard the music and headed in the direction of the corner pub. The guidebook Charlie had devoured on the plane wasn't much help now she was on the ground, and Google maps could only tell her so much. Besides, she would much prefer to discover Sydney organically than have a predetermined path. She'd lived with predetermination for the last twenty-eight years and it was nice to be spontaneous for a change. There was no one checking up on her or making sure she stayed within the boundaries. It was her emancipation and it was only going to last a week so she intended to wring every single last drop out of it.

Charlie pushed through the door and breathed in the sound and chaos of the crowd. She soaked it up like a sponge. Charlie didn't care if she looked like a country bumpkin just off the bus as she looked around her with big eyes trying to take everything in. She squeezed her way to the bar and ordered a Cosmo, just like the girls from Sex and the City.

Drink in hand she turned and tried to fight her way back through the crowd without spilling the pink concoction in her hand. She made it almost all the way and was just lifting the glass to her lips when someone bumped into her from behind, causing her to spill the entire thing down her front.

"Sorry," came a distracted apology. She looked over her shoulder to reply but whoever had bumped into her was lost in the crush of bodies.

Charlie looked down at herself. Her new dress now sported a bright pink stain that caused it to stick to her skin. She felt a little like the kid who dropped their ice-cream after just one lick. The cocktail had cost her eighteen bucks, which she had been prepared to pay for the experience, but not to wear it.

"Hey, are you okay?"

Charlie looked up into the chocolate coloured eyes of the most beautiful man she had ever seen. She could even forgive him for the scruffy whiskers and man-bun because that English accent smoothed over any fashion faux-pas he'd made.

"Um, yeah, sure. I'm fine."

He quirked an eyebrow and she felt her cheeks flush.

"Can I buy you a replacement?" he asked.

"Oh no," she said, shaking her head. "You don't need to do that. I'm fine, I promise."

"I don't mind," he said. "I'm heading to the bar anyway."

Charlie took a breath. What would Amelia do? This trip was all about stepping out of her comfort zone so, instead of declining again, she channelled Amelia, smiled, and nodded. "Yeah, okay," she said.

He smiled back at her and her breath caught in her chest. "I have that table over there in the corner if you want to have a seat. I'll bring the drinks over."

"Sure, yeah, okay" she said, nodding again like a bobblehead.

He winked at her before turning back to the crowd in front of the bar and Charlie made her way over to the table he'd indicated. She sat down and grabbed some napkins out of the dispenser to try and mop up the spilled drink from her dress.

While she waited for the stranger to return, she tried to memorise everything about the moment so she could relive it all later. Charlie was determined to store up as many memories as she could, while she could. There was no telling when she would have another chance and the memories she made now would have to sustain her.

"Here you go," he said, setting her drink down in front of her. "Cosmopolitan, right?"

"Perfect," she said. "I'm Charlie, I mean Charlotte, I mean..." she shook her head. "My name's Charlotte but everyone calls me Charlie."

He grinned at her. "My name's Kit," he said, extending his hand across the table to her. "It's nice to meet you Charlie."

She took his hand and shook it. Her palm tingled with the connection and her eyes went to his in surprise. "It's nice to meet you too," she whispered.

MEETING THE WIZARD OF OZ
is available now

A C K N O W L E D G M E N T S

What can I say? I wrote this book because I needed something fun and light. Of all the characters that I've written, Georgie is probably the closest to me. Believe it or not, most of my characters have some part of me in them - even the male ones - but Georgie was different. Georgie is who I'd most likely be if my life hadn't taken the twists and turns that it has.

For those of you who actually read these acknowledgements, I'll let you in on a little secret...when I was creating Connor there was one actor who I couldn't get out of my mind. Chris Hemsworth. I couldn't help it. Connor just seemed to become Chris. So thank you Chris Hemsworth (one of my two favourite Chris', the other being Chris Pine).

While we're doing the thank yous I have to thank, as always, my husband who supports me and encourages me every single day and who understands that some days I have to sit at a computer all day, or read all day (in the name of research) or watched romantic movies to fill my creative well. He is always my leading man.

Also thank you to Kathryn for your constant encouragement

and your enthusiasm for my books. It's like having my own personal cheerleader and I love it and you! Mwah!

Thank you too to Brooke for reaching out to me and offering me your incredible talent and your time to edit my writing. I always thought I was pretty good with that stuff, but you have shown me how far off the mark I was! You have made my writing better and I cannot express just how much I appreciate you.

To all my readers, thank you! I hope you enjoyed this little bit of light-hearted fun. I am planning more Bookish Book Club Novellas, I'm just not sure where they will fit in my production schedule, so keep your eyes peeled... or better yet, join my New Release Mailing List!

Have you read The Young Royals series?

Book 1 - A Royal Engagement

Despite being the second child of the King and Queen of Merveille, Alyssabeth thought that if she kept a low profile she could stay out of the media's glaring spotlight and live a relatively normal life. That was until her father, the King, and her brother, the Crown Prince, was both killed in a hunting accident.

Her dream of joining the UN was no more and instead she needed to return to the small European country of her birth to pick up where her father and brother left off. Her Harvard degree in International Relations is forfeit and in it's place she must become Queen, that was if the misogynistic Parliament can see past their prejudices.

Not much had changed in the small country in her four year

absence, but there are two noticeable differences. Her brother's two best friends Will Darkly and Jordan Wicks have grown up into two very intriguing men. Jordan practically swept her off her feet from the moment she stepped off the plane, but Will's more reserved, darkly intense interest in her gave her tingles.

Alyssa wasn't sure she was cut out to be Queen, but she knew that she wanted to do her father and brother proud, so she was willing to give it her best shot, even if it meant going toe to toe with Parliament. And then there was the small matter of her needing to be married in order to fulfil her birthright and take her place as the Head of State.

Book 2 - A Royal Entanglement

On the day of the new Queen's coronation, a man from Lady Alexandra's past turns up unannounced in Merveille. Lord Frédéric intercepts him and discovers that Alex had left this man at the altar six months ago and now he was here to claim her.

Alex hasn't told anyone the real reason she left everything she had worked so hard for in the States to move to Merveille and take up the position of Queen Alyssa's personal assistant. But now the main reason for her flight from the US has turned up on the palace's doorstep and she is backed into a corner. The only person that she can think of to help her is Freddie, but she's worried that getting too close to him might just do more harm than good.

The last thing Freddie wants is to get entangled with a woman. He liked to keep his options open, but now that he has returned to Merveille for good, his mother is trying her damnedest to get him married off and producing the next Bingham heir. When Alex asks for his help, he is only too eager to help her and maybe get his mother off his back in the process. He never expected to fall for her.

Book 3 - A Royal Entrapment

The Queen is getting married and Priscilla is required to work alongside the Lord Chancellor, Dominique, to ensure that the whole affair goes off without a hitch and that they don't, unwittingly, start World War Three. The only problem is that Priscilla finds Dominique insufferable and Dom isn't all that enamoured with Priscilla either.

When Priscilla's sister, Bianca, falls for Dominique's brother, Louis, the two young lovers hatch a plot to ensure that they can spend time together, but it means that Dom has to pretend to be interested in Priscilla and get her to date him.

The more time they spend together, the more Dom and Priscilla start to like each other, except that now Dom is caught in a difficult spot...should he tell Priscilla that he only asked her out because his brother wanted to date her sister, or should he keep quiet and hope she doesn't find out?

Book 4 - A Royal Expectation

Lady Jeanette Bower had always known what her life was going to look like. It had been drummed into her since she was a little girl. She would marry a titled gentleman and make him a splendid wife who was above reproach. It was what her mother had always wanted for her and Lady Jeanette always did what her mother wanted her to do. She was a good girl. The only problem was, Lady Jeanette didn't expect a six foot four Australian with sparkling tawny coloured eyes and a mischievous grin to walk into her life and show her that there was perhaps another path for her to take.

Drew Taylor had just landed his dream job and the fact that it was half way around the world from his meddling mother was just icing on the cake. He never expected to be swept off his feet by a woman on a hot pink Ducati. A woman who also happened to be one of the queen's ladies in waiting. And then there was the complication of the viscount she was supposed to marry. How could a cane farmer's son from tropical Queensland compete with a man who could give Lady Jeanette the title she had always wanted? He couldn't, but that wouldn't stop him from trying.

Book 5 - A Royal Elopement

Lady Meredith Bingham thought that she had her life sorted. She was a member of the royal guard - an elite security team tasked with protecting the queen of Merveille. She was also close personal friends with the queen and part of her inner circle - the ladies in waiting. But then her mother had to go and ruin it all. Lady Caroline Bingham was sick of her daughter fooling around and playing soldier. She thought it was high time her daughter got serious about her future and found herself a suitable husband. With the duke pulling double duty as the country's prime minister, it was only right that his daughter start acting like a proper daughter of nobility. Much to Meredith's chagrin, the queen agrees that Meredith must step down from her post.

Prince Christophe Kostopolous was a prince in exile. For the last ten years he had been living under the pseudonym of Jamie Kosta, and for the last seven years he has been part of the royal guard. Very few people knew his true identity, but that was all about to change. The people he had been hiding from all these years have found him and he may finally have his chance to reclaim his rightful place on the throne of his small island nation of Kalopsia. The only problem is, he has fallen for a certain duke's daughter and she has no idea who he really is.

Book 6 - A Royal Embarrassment

Savannah has a secret...a secret that could cost her everything she's been working for.

Coming to Merveille and taking up a position as one of Queen Alyssa's ladies in waiting hadn't been part of Savannah Rousseau's plan, but she wasn't going to turn down the opportunity when it came her way. The daughter of an impoverished viscount, Savannah had nothing to lose and everything to gain by being included amongst the new queen's entourage...as long as no one found out about her secret.

Savannah loved her son. Archer was the sun and moon of her life, but being a single mother would mean instant disqualification from the ladies in waiting. So she hid him from the queen and her new friends...for two years. Now someone had stumbled upon her secret and Savannah would do anything to ensure that she didn't become a royal embarrassment.

Jed Fairchild came to Merveille to escape his own scandal and the last thing he wanted was to be embroiled in another. Finding out about the young boy and impoverished viscount that Savannah had stashed in the abandoned hunting cabins was a complication that he didn't need. Being attracted to the hot-tempered lady in waiting was another. All Jed wanted was to live a simple life working with his horses and ignoring the rest of the world, but with Savannah in his life and the inquisitive Archer following him like his very own shadow, the quiet life was the last thing Jed had...and maybe it wasn't really what he wanted after all.

Book 6.5 - A Very Royal Christmas

Lady Georgina Darkly, the newly titled

Duchess of Pemberton, did not need one more thing to deal with the week before Christmas. The temperature was dropping alarmingly, a snow storm had been predicted, the milk tanks in the dairy were close to freezing and there was a leak in her bedroom roof. To top it all off Clarabelle, the cow that had a mischievous streak a mile wide, had escaped the confines of the barn and could very well freeze to death if Georgie didn't find her soon. The absolute very last thing she needed was an arrogant, stubborn, wealthy, and undeniably *gorgeous* Italian to turn up on her doorstep in need of rescuing.

Leonardo Ricci, youngest son of one of Italy's wealthiest families did not want to be stuck in the middle of a snow storm in a country barely more than the size of a postage stamp. He wanted to be with his friends in Milan not suffering through a stilted family Christmas with his parents. When a cow appeared in the middle of the road and caused his beautiful Ferrari to careen out of control into a snow bank, he honestly didn't think his day could get any worse...and then he met the Duchess. She was opinionated, stubborn, far too capable for her own good, stunningly beautiful, and immune to his charms. They had nothing in common and if she hadn't rescued him then he probably would never have given her another thought. But then they got stuck together in her rundown mansion with no electricity and no phones...and that's when the sparks really started to fly.

Book 7 - A Royal Enticement

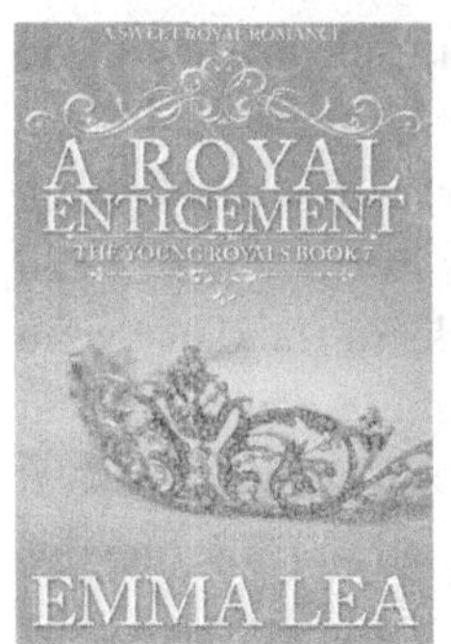

Lady Margaret de la Fontaine was the forgotten lady in waiting. She didn't mind...most of the time. She liked working with Lady Savannah and the others and believed whole-heartedly in what the queen was trying to achieve in their small country of Merveille. She just wished that someone would notice her, just once.

Queen Alyssa's ladies in waiting had, one by one, met and fallen in love with their dream partners, all except Margaret, not that anybody had given her single status another thought. That didn't mean she didn't also wish for someone to love, but she wasn't holding her breath, especially since her best friend, Lady Hadley Winchester, was now part of the ladies in waiting. It seemed the newest member of the group was a hit with everyone, including the queen, which was great but once again left Margaret as the wallflower.

Until Brín.

Brín noticed the sweet wee Maggie standing against the wall while everyone else at the ball danced and chatted. He felt a kinship with her, even across the room and sought her out for a little bit of harmless flirting. He was supposed to be checking out the candidates for his arranged marriage, but he really wasn't keen on the whole idea. He understood his responsibility as the lost heir of a broken down estate that was haemorrhaging money, but he didn't really see himself as the marrying kind...and even if he did, he'd want to do it for love, not money.

Brín was immediately taken with Lady Margaret, but alas, she was not the debutante his advisors had picked out for him. That honour went to Maggie's best friend, Lady Hadley. But what was a newly minted earl to do when he had the livelihoods of several staff and families to look after? Not to mention, if he didn't find a solution he may very well lose the estate and the title that went with it.

ABOUT THE AUTHOR

Emma Lea is a barista, artist, cook, mother and wife. She lives on the beautiful Sunshine Coast in Queensland, Australia with her wonderful husband. She has two beautiful, grown-up sons, a dog and a cat (both of which are female because, hey, we needed to balance all that testosterone!)

She is a ferocious reader with eclectic tastes and has always wanted to write, but never had the opportunity due to one reason or another (excuses, really) until finally taking the bullet between her teeth in 2014 and just making herself do it.

She loves to write stories with heart and a message and believes in strong female characters who do not necessarily have to be aggressive to show their strength.

If you enjoyed reading this book, please share the love by leaving a review and telling your friends!

To connect with Emma Lea
www.emmaleaauthor.com

THANKS

Thank you for reviewing this book and recommending it to your friends and family.
Honest reviews are important for authors and I appreciate the time you have taken to share your thoughts.

This is Emma Lea's complete book library at time of publication, but more books are coming out all the time. Find out every time Emma releases a book by going to her website (www.emmaleaauthor.com) and signing up for her Newsletter.

SWEET ROMANCES

These are romantic tales without the bedroom scenes and the swearing, but that doesn't mean they're boring!

The Young Royals

A Royal Engagement

Lord Darkly

A Royal Entanglement

A Royal Entrapment

A Royal Expectation

A Royal Elopement

A Royal Embarrassment

A Very Royal Christmas

A Royal Enticement

Bookish Book Club Novellas

Meeting Prince Charming

Meeting the Wizard of Oz

Meeting Santa Claus

SWEET & SEXY ROMANCES

In my Sweet & Sexy Romances I turn up the heat with a little bit of sexy.

No swearing, or very minimal swearing, and brief, tasteful and not too graphic bedroom scenes.

Love, Money & Shoes Series

Walk of Shame

Standalone Novels

Amnesia

HOT & SEXY ROMANCES

Hot & Spicy Romances turn the heat way up. They contain swearing and sexy scenes and the characters get hot under the collar.

Recommended for 18+ readers

TGIF Series

Girl Friday

Black Friday

Good Friday

Twelve Days

Twelve Days of Christmas - Her Side of the Story

Twelve Days of Christmas - His Side of the Story

Collins Bay Series

Last Call

The Christmas Stand-Off

Standalone Novels

Learning to Breathe

Romantic Suspense

Hide & Seek

<u>TOO HOT TO HANDLE ROMANCES</u>

These are definitely 18+ reads and contain graphic sex scenes and high level swearing – not for the faint of heart

<u>The Young Billionaires</u>

The Billionaire Stepbrother

The Billionaire Daddy

The Billionaire Muse

The Billionaire Replacement

The Billionaire Trap

Christmas with the Billionaire

<u>Music & Lyrics</u>

Rock Star

Songbird

Strings

Sticks

Symphony

<u>The Playbook Series</u>

In Like Flynn

Manscaping

<u>Serendipity Trilogy</u>

The Wrong Girl

The Right Girl (coming soon)

The Only Girl (coming soon)

Made in the USA
Monee, IL
07 July 2026